Harm None

GAY LYNCH

HEMBURY
—BOOKS—

Contents

Harm None by Dr Gay Lynch

Copyright Gay Lynch ©

Hembury Books 2025

hemburybooks.com.au

info@hemburybooks.com

Paperback ISBN - 9781763807747

Ebook ISBN - 9781763807730

A catalogue record for this book is available at the National Library of Australia.

Quotes from Arthur Miller's *The Crucible: a Play in Four Acts* (1953) taken from the Penguin Classics Orange Collection (New York: Penguin Books, 2016).

Praise for Gay Lynch

"*Harm None* reads like a spell: sharp and sinister, and deeply evocative of the early 2000s." – Margot McGovern

"Gripping and beautifully written – *Harm None* casts a spell you won't want to break.
Mysterious, unsettling and utterly captivating." – Sharon Kernot

"In vivid relatable prose, *Harm None* tells the story of Garnet's search for truth in a world where family and friends are unreliable while hormones, homework and risk-taking stretch and blur the boundaries." – Anne Casey-Hardy

About the Author

Dr Gay Lynch writes essays, novels, hybrid memoir pieces, academic papers, book reviews and short stories on unceded Bunurong land, part of the Kulin nation. She is an adjunct lecturer in creative writing and English at Flinders University.

In 2005, she published *Cleanskin*, her first novel, mentored as a SAWC (South Australian Writers Centre) prize, by Eva Horning, then-Eva Sallis. In 2019, she published her second novel *Unsettled*, mentored by Irish writer Niall Williams. Her essays and stories have appeared in *Best Australian Stories*, *Meanjin* and *Griffith Review*, among other publications.

Lynch has been short and long listed for FISH Flash and Short Memoir prizes. In 2023, she chaired and presented sessions for the Australian Short Story Festival (ASSF), the International Conference on Short Story in English (ICSSE), and launched her new work in *Pratic: a Magazine of Contemporary Writing* for Asia-Pacific Writers and Translators (APWT) at the Ubud Readers and Writers Festival. In 2024, she won the Creative Prose Prize 1st Prize for AAALS (American Association Australasian Literary Studies).

She has also worked as a journal editor, teacher-librarian, school coordinator for the May Gibbs Writers in Residence Program and workshop leader. Her engagement with middle-school students sparked her interest in teen/young adult and coming-of-age novels, with their authentic voices, focus on personal growth and ethical issues, and redemptive leanings.

Originally shortlisted for the Adelaide Festival Literary Award for an Unpublished Manuscript in 2002, *Harm None* is her first young-adult novel.

Chapter One

'AN IT HARM NONE DO WHAT YE WILL.'

As winter deepened, some lines of thought untangled, and others snarled.
It became impossible to grasp where harm fell and who caused it.

EARLY MARCH 2003

Intent on reaching the river, Garnet's mother rushed past sprawling pairs of crab-apple trees and feral-pink oleanders. On the edge, she stood on one leg and then the other, to upend her rubber boots, and shake their contents onto the path. A paisley shawl had slid from her shoulders and trailed behind her, and she gathered it up, clasped it hard against her chest, then hurried along the bank into the shadows.

Alerted by yellow-tailed black cockatoos threading the sky, her daughter had first observed her mother in silhouette. 'Mother, do not hide for hours, I may or may not miss you.'

She imagined her halting beneath a willow tree, head cocked, straining to hear distant birds' wings or some taunting she had scrivened in her brain.

'Raven – who is my father?' she yelled pointlessly after her.

Only once ever had her mother showed enough curiosity to turn and shout, 'Why...? Do you need?'

Few mothers parented with burning oils, lit candles, herbal tinctures and flowers, mirrors and bowls of warm water. Raven was sweet. Little point in moaning that she was kind of disconnected — she'd planted a poison garden, for fuck's sake — with everything lined up in rows, an obsessive symmetry that led all the way to the river.

Garnet's grandmother Ebba, who lived with them, said the plants were for healing as well as for eating, but hinted at 'episodes' when Raven had technically stacked it and moved into an eastern suburbs private hospital to get her shit together. Most of the time, Raven was a dreamy absence, a shadow wafting out of the house to tend her garden or walk by the river. Monday to Friday afternoons she worked in a second-hand bookshop, traded hard-covers, poured coffee, and nodded serenely at the couple of women who discoursed there about human genomes, the critical state of sand piling, the nature of information and the death of the novel. After school, if Garnet missed the bus home, she walked towards the shop to grab a ride in her mother's ancient Peugeot.

Now fifteen, she held happiness hard to herself, encoded it in every cell of her changing body. When Raven came to say goodnight, head bowed, plucking at the bedcovers, the pungent smell of lavender wafted out from her neck. Bewildered and sleep-fuzzy, Garnet liked how her mother's voice seemed imbued with strange love. But hated how when she reached up to touch her, Raven spoiled everything by raving a litany: 'Aconite, belladonna, buckthorn, buttercup, cannabis, cinquefoil, foxglove, hellebore, henbane, monkshood, rue, scotch broom, tansy.' And then smiled, dreamily. Grandmother Ebba's influence, perhaps, or her encyclopaedic brain.

For hours, her mother watched clouds. When restless and seeking, she could hear the fall of a leaf. Or so she said. When Ebba poked at their evening fires with gnarled sticks, she offered Garnet more pieces of the triangulated puzzle of their matriarchal family. Garnet dropped these facts into files named 'Paisley,' 'Plants' and 'Journal.' Never mind the head-fuck file titled 'Mother.'

If Ebba left them for the next world, Garnet wanted to become keeper of the secrets. Unlike Raven – who let everything good slip through her fingers. Garnet wanted peace and quiet, and wondered, when she photographed Raven's twin plantings, why her mother placed such restraint on a garden, especially when she yearned so much to be loose and free.

Which path should a daughter take when her mother tugged at her hands in the wind? Ebba identified as country? Was Raven safer here in the valley than when she disappeared down city streets, face damp, pupils enlarged, clothes awry?

A rosemary hedge divided their small river cottage from their neighbours. Between and beyond sprawled a cottage garden, densely planted with food for the body and succour for the soul. Rows of catkins, daphne and oleander trees struggled in pairs along the path towards the river. During spring, foxgloves and lavender bushes frothed at their feet. One of the holy yews had given up the ghost in a drought year and no amount of water would coax it back. A curse, perhaps, rebelling against its foreign and toxic setting.

The second cottage had lain empty for years, until the three of them had almost forgotten the possibility of another resident. Then, in this most recent autumn, when days took longer to warm, and the chill rushed in at dusk, a tall man nosed his silver Jag into the driveway and braked on the gravel.

From upstairs, Garnet watched him slide like oil from behind the wheel of his car. He wore a black leather jacket and pants, more suited to a motorbike than to a car. A heavy silver chain dangled from his pocket. At his heel sat one of those killer – well ill-treated or neglected – dogs, that drag babies out of prams, crunch toddlers in back yards, and latch onto the legs of war veterans. Though right now the dog looked milder than its owner. Dark hair cropped short and fake blonde tips must be flaky at his age. Ditto the silver moon that glinted from his left ear.

The new neighbour stared hard at Garnet's window, as if he had picked up her scent. Or perhaps she should stop reading the hot books her friend Cody lent her, now hidden at the back of her wardrobe. Looping the dog's chain over a metal upright, the man wove his way through the gap in the hedge on his way to his front door. Out of the corner of her eye, Garnet watched a pale, thin sylph in Indian cotton slide home through the garden, and wave vaguely in the man's direction. Her heart sank. Why did her mother pay attention to all the wrong things? Ebba would say the autumn equinox unsettled everyone and everything: mothering, daughtering, light, dark. Mabon madness disturbed the very air.

Garnet bent to document this surprising development in her digital diary, but first leant forward to flick open her photo program. Eyes and cheeks bulging, she rotated her zombie face clockwise.

'A most refreshing nine hours of shuteye,' she captioned it. 'Today is the first day of my new life. Living next door to a man.'

She saved the pic, and her computer crashed. She rebooted — rocked on her chair, bad girl — head thrown back, her fingers aggravating the hole between the legs of her pjs as she waited for desktop icons to reappear. Damned if she wanted her mother to know the secret pleasure she took in her body. None of her business. Her journal remained hidden — well-hidden — away from glancing eyes. A hex on mothers — especially Raven — who would suck your soul through a screen.

Once, there had been a pink, plastic-coated birthday journal with a tinny, bendy key and the words 'My Diary' scrawled across the front. Garnet hadn't been smart enough — she was a kid, for Gaia's sake — to know how a breach of privacy could wound. One night, as she dozed in front of the television, it had slipped from her lap. She bet, bet *anything*, that quite composed, Raven had dipped into it with no qualms and afterwards put it back on the kitchen table.

'I didn't read it,' her mother said during their argument through the open loo door. 'Well, anything interesting.'

'Bullshit!' Garnet cried out, peeling trails of wallpaper. 'On both counts.' When she came out, she wrote a blood-red biro note and left it under Raven's pillow:

I hate you, Mother – you suck.

. . .

After that she lost interest in baiting adults over their lies and threw the pink book into the river. Garnet would manage everything better than her mother, because Ebba was mostly on her side.

Speaking of which, her grandmother called up the stairs.

'You'll miss the bus if you don't hurry up. Are you dressed?'

Garnet half glanced at her computer screen, from which an image of a boy stared back into her room, tears glittering in his eyes. Her hand shook. She'd seen him before. Just an illusion, like the *Magic Eye* book Ebba gave her for her sixth birthday. Eventually she had learned to relax her vision, and the little coloured squares reorganised themselves into images. The trick was to forget the old way of looking and concentrate on finding the hidden picture.

Just like that, the image of the boy slid away, his edges blurry, then coalescing. Ebba said that there were some days when everyone felt double, and on other days incomplete. Garnet's heart hammered beneath her nightgown. Yes Ebba, time to exit the dark, dark place where half an hour ago she been happily torrenting music, and take a shower.

Peering around her bedroom curtains, Garnet decided the next-door cottage looked shut up. Part of her hoped the man had gone, and part of her felt let down. The valley was dull. Dull, dull. Fog drifted through the back yard, lingering over summer stubble and settling heavily over the river. Crows whipped across the sky in groups of three or four, business-like, planning winter. Parched and tired, gums creaked, their upper bows leafless.

Breakfast, teeth, face, Docs, books dropped into her pink string bag, she waited ankles crossed for the yellow bus. Dress code got her down. She poked her finger through a tear in her fishnets and swished her black crepe skirt over it. Ebba said they couldn't make her wear school uniform, or kick her out because of it. Kids were legally entitled to an education. Some teachers cared about Garnet, but, every morning, others who would rather play power games than teach gave her the run-around.

'You are not complying with the dress code. Do I need to remind you of the specifics? Please present yourself at the front office.'

After a few notes home the school seemed quite discouraged. For a while Raven had written politely back:

To Whom it May Concern,
    Thank you, once more, for bringing this matter to my attention. Garnet has a problem with blue stretch fabrics. Please let me know if she fails to meet any other of your expectations.
    Yours sincerely,
    Raven Southwood

But then her mother got sick of the school's interruptions to her very important life and wrote:

Please stop ringing me. There is nothing I can do to help you with your problem.

After a while, the halfway reasonable teachers got off Garnet's case, and she drifted into her classes in sage-green net or whatever and opened her books. David Drakon, her English teacher, had never breathed a word.

The tech teacher – up himself totally – 'The dress code thing... between you and me, I'm over it,' he whispered. 'Open your report and make sure it's correctly formatted. Then go and help the others.'

Asking her to troubleshoot gave him points for affirmative action. She cruised around the terminals under his instruction: correctile-dysfunction, according to Ebba. Likely technophobic girls made him puke. Nice try, to email her extra work after hours. Power was the point. Offloading his work on a kid in pretence of her benefit.

Every day, the bus deposited Garnet and all the other valley kids at the school gate where her BF waited for her. Cody looked like an angel, plaits woven around her head in a neat coronet, because her mother had once been crowned Miss Riverina. Even though Cody was a year older, they both had duxed their classes all the way from Year Four, Primary School, when Garnet had arrived from the city. Still seated quietly at the back of the class, heads ducked together, arms shielding work from the boys across the aisle. They had lately given up tickling each other's legs beneath the desk, for the same reason. Getting caught, kiss of death. Boys always made girls pay.

Cody's rebellious state had arrived with her pimples, Garnet's inbuilt. The first fifteen minutes before the bell rang, they spent under the pepper tree-fringed oval, to purify Cody's system with smoke, to get rid of home goodness instilled by her parents, who were fierce, straight, and sweet, and cared about dress codes and old-fashioned values. Yet Ebba believed in Cody and allowed the girls tightly governed sleepovers. Had things changed recently? Last time, Garnet hadn't been allowed to stay over at her friend's.

Garnet and Cody had joined the messenger service at the same time but kept their friend lists small. Neither fancied people their own age. And they didn't do personal photos. Better not to wade through pages of drivel, laced with profanities and sexual obsessions, in open chat rooms. Better not to waste time with some thirteen-year-old illiterate locked in his bedroom with a sweaty mouse, a shitload of acne and a fantasy about being a deviant.

No one on Garnet and Cody's lists could be called a close mate. Zane, a Year Twelve boy, had set up a group with two other boys in his year and few girls. Cody got the nod from her cousin Mick, who was Zane's mate, and then she pulled in Garnet. Lyndon Kershaw was a Year Twelve brain, and quieter than the mall at midnight. Kendra and Daisy were much the same — kept a low profile and lived in each other's knickers. Very discreet. Nobody remembered much about Zane before that.

They'd made an undeclared joint decision not to yap their faces off at school. Just nod in the quadrangle — keep an eye on each other as they manoeuvred in their respective groups. When someone jumped Lyndon behind the bike shed, over his physics test result, A+, Garnet and Cody had gone in for him, launched themselves into the fracas, at risk of being called *dumb bitches*, nothing too precious. Hooting like hyenas they flung their arms and legs about. By then a couple of Lyndon's mates arrived with the duty teacher and everyone sloped off. School was worse than *Village of the Damned*.

Garnet's sporadic overachievements in class were ignored because she looked a bit feral and posed no social threat. Lyndon mainly kept under the radar. Two years older and taller than the girls, he, Zane and Mick had all cleared puberty. Garnet liked the *zzz* of power when their eyes rested with instinctive if veiled joy on her bits. She could wait to see what happened. Cody could not.

Most days, bookshop trade was quiet, and when Garnet and Cody arrived at the shop after school, they invariably found Raven curled up like a comma, on a stool behind the counter, her dark hair curtaining Genet or Flaubert or Proust. Today, Coupland's *Microserf*. Did her reading choices mean much, or had she plucked from a pile of books dumped on the counter?

When she noticed her at all, Raven treated Cody with studied respect. She smiled as if half-absent, played with her hair and said vague random things like, 'The echidna is back. Salmon Rushdie is worried about the Bulger killers.' Or, 'Not enough wind is worse than too much.' Mostly she sounded a few years out of date. Cody must have thought Raven nuts and then some. Her mother was more normal, like a nervy terrier, who jumped them at the door with, 'How was *today*?' Unaccustomed to such precise attention, Garnet trawled through her memories of the day's experiences, searching for an acceptable contribution.

'Umm ... no-one pinged me for the dress code.'

Cody's mum blinked. Probably wished she hadn't asked. Probably found Raven's style of parenting incomprehensible. Fair call on both counts.

The day that Garnet first glimpsed the neighbour in the Jag had been no different to a hundred others. Cody kissed her cheek and waved goodbye and Garnet lumped her bag home from the bookshop.

After closing, Raven drove Garnet the fifteen kilometres along the river road to the cottage.

'Plato believed the body was a vehicle for the soul,' she proffered.

'What*ever*!' Garnet slouched against the passenger door, feet on the dash, and fiddled with her phone. 'Who was that guy this morning?'

'This morning?' Raven looked vague, but not every byte was a bit, or legit.

'The black leather dude.' Garnet twiddled the radio dial with her holey-stockinged toe and unleashed a load of static.

'Garnet! Don't do that. Put your feet down.' Raven put her hand to her head. 'Didn't I tell you? He's renting the other cottage.'

'Has he got a horse?'

'No. Why?'

'Random thought. Delete.' Garnet wound down the window and dangled her arm. 'I'm hot.'

'My ears are ringing. Please put it up.'

Garnet flipped her fingers in the wind.

'His name is Branwell Kershaw, and we never thought the owners'd rent out that cottage, so don't you let him spoil anything. Take care of yourself.'

Garnet laughed. 'That's very funny, Mother. Thank you for caring.' She sighed and bent over her schoolbag, hauling out a dog-eared text. 'Do you know *The Crucible*?'

'The play?'

'What else?'

'Read it years ago.'

'Must be ancient. We're studying it for English.'

'Remind me of the basic plot.'

'Weird religious community in America. Girls work like slaves and the men pontificate until one of them bonks his wife's maid and, just like happens now, she loses her job. But he's picked the wrong chick. Abigail counter-accuses everyone in his orbit... mass slaughter ensues or equiv...'

'Yes, I remember. I haven't thought about it for years. A perfect storm. Salem would have been dangerous for women who had minds of their own.'

'Hrm... thinking about yourself, are you?' Garnet tries to keep a straight face.

'I'm remembering a character in the play, killed for reading too much. Husband realised too late that in complaining, he'd sent his woman to the gallows.'

It is my third wife, Sir; I never had no wife that be so taken with books, and I thought to find the cause of it, d'y'see, but it were no witch I blamed her for. He is openly weeping. I have broken charity with the woman...

'Murder and mayhem. On repeat.' Raven sighed. 'Of course, he regrets his nastiness.'

'I haven't got that far yet. Just regurgitated Drako's synopsis in more simple language so you'd understand.'

Her mother poked her in the side. 'Very funny. I'll dig out my old copy.'

Garnet twiddled the dial to make the radio kick back in at one hundred decibels.

When they swung into the driveway, both cottages looked empty. Ebba worked long hours and came home late. Raven toasted rye bread and disappeared. Garnet followed suit, went to her room, and logged on with butter and vegemite oozing through her fingers.

A bloody spider had draped its web across her monitor. Very pushy. Not half as pushy as the night one of her redback mates bit Garnet on the leg in bed. Ebba rang the doctor, who advised to keep an eye on her, apply ice. Most people didn't die, he said. Should do stand-up comedy. Garnet's leg had throbbed for hours.

This day, she took off her shoe and used it to pull the web away to the left. The spider scurried up the main drag-line and stared down at her.

'I know you took forever building that, but my rules. If you're going to mess about while I'm at school, don't crap on my hardware.'

Who could kill a spider after reading *Charlotte's Web*? Aged seven, Garnet had bawled her head off. She would have to put this one in a pot for a day – thanks, Ebba – whether it brought on a storm or not. Usually captivity quietened them, and afterwards they busied themselves at the back of the wardrobe. For days. Ebba said spiders were associated with creativity and imagination. But this one. Such a drone, building and rebuilding her web.

It was early. Normal families were probably at tennis coaching. The essay on *The Crucible* wasn't due until the end of Week 8. Garnet cruised around looking for good sites. Usually, she could find chapter summaries and character descriptions, but if you could read a text yourself you were better off. Half of Garnet's class couldn't — read, that is. No prizes for guessing which half. She'd have to ask Raven about the critical mass of illiterate boys and then prepare for the Big Bang. In America, boys took their guns or blades to school.

Ting

    Zane: Does it worry you that your mail sits on a massive hard drive?

    Garnet: Why? Are you paranoid?

    Zane: Definition of paranoid?

    Garnet: Yup? Hit me with it.

    Zane: Someone in possession of all the facts.

    Garnet: I don't think so! What are you doing tonight? :-)

    Zane: Locating and lifting a useful essay on *The Crucible*. Have you found a good one?

    Garnet: Haven't looked.

    Zane: Might just search for music.

    Garnet: Are you sad again?

    Zane: No, why?

    Garnet: You don't sound grumpy. I didn't mean anything. Just your Dad, you know.

    Zane: your space, my space, you out.

A car door slammed.

· · ·

Garnet: Something's happening. SYL.

She rushed to the window. Mr Branwell Renshaw. Boring — to perve on an old man – but off the hook with Zane. Dressed in tight black track pants and skivvy, and club-styled boots, the neighbour ferried crates with slat fronts from his vehicle and trailer to his back door. He looked South American, maybe Columbian. Probably brought his guinea pigs with him. Was that racist? But then what about his weird, witchy name? In English, Branwell meant raven, like her mother's, just a bird; but also 'broom,' and in Irish, Branwell sounded more Abraham in the Bible. She'd looked it up.

Garnet pushed her head between the bedposts and deep into the window recess to get a better look at him as he unhitched a trailer stacked with wood. Not logs for his fire, but timber cut in building lengths.

A boobook owl persistently called from across the river. Willows ruffled in the wind. Ebba said they brought blessings and guarded the home. Raven said they choked the river. That Ebba should have more sense. It was difficult to know where her garden began and her mother's ended. What would *he* think of Ebba's herb patch — planted out in a five-pointed star — earth, air, fire and water, and the fifth element that bound them all?

'What are you doing?' Raven drifted into the room, worrying with her fingers at her amber necklace, her silver eyebrow ring standing up in conference with her frown as she moved towards the window.

'Reading *The Crucible*, if you must know. *Is the accuser always holy now?*'

Raven smiled and ducked her head. '*Were they born this morning as clean as God's fingers?... little crazy children...*'

Garnet manipulated her foot to gather up the textbook spine up at the rumpled end of her bed. 'Abigail is seventeen, Mother. Nor am I a child.'

At the sound of a car door banging, her mother stared soundlessly through the window, down into the yard, and then moved away, softly touching three fingers to Garnet's forehead as she passed on her way to the door.

'Stay focussed,' she whispered. She sounded almost sensible.

Next week, she could go crazy, jump on a plane to Melbourne, fill up all her credit cards in an afternoon, fly back, party all night, bring home very strange men. Why hadn't Zane's father Dr Andrew tried her on Ritalin? Half of Garnet's class took it. Dispensed by the same parents who panicked over 'the drug problem'. Years ago, when Garnet and Ebba visited Raven in hospital, the room had buzzed with noisy people passing tokes.

Raven's downswings were hardcore. She stopped eating, spent days in bed or become a thin, pale, shadow floating round the house. Better or worse? Ebba meditated, using her daughter's hair or a photograph, to visualise her healing. Covered the water from a chalice with a cloth and left it out all night. In the mornings, she encouraged her to sip herbal antidotes. They sat at the table, cinnamon incense swirling round them as they talked and cried together.

Waiting for dinner, hungry, Garnet slouched around. If they were lucky, Raven would chuck a few wild weeds on a plate. Most nights they ate together. Ebba worked late, counselling at a city women's centre called Sappho where she picked up clients referred on by government agencies and staffed with a few busy, broader-minded doctors. Women walked in off the street to start courses on Reiki and self-defence and unloaded all their problems at the same time.

Ebba stayed calm but complex and wore stone beads in multiples of nine. Garnet imagined her connecting with the battle-scarred and weary; she bet that they stared at her granny's wild white hair, her black suit, and her gentle eyes, one disconcertingly green, the other blue, and then tried harder to survive.

Maybe that was why Raven was highly strung. Ebba had probably given her heaps of space in the teen years and then watched in horror as the last screw slipped sideways in her daughter's brain. Would smacking have been more effective? Raven had been a young mother — early thirties — but offered no cosy stories about the birthing experience, soft lights, music, or the word 'love'. Ebba and her circle of women would have been present. But they didn't talk about it.

At about the age of six Garnet had first thought to ask her mother, 'Where the hell is my father?' Raven had raised her eyebrow at the language. It had been a bit vague, the explanation. Something about timing, lost contact — overseas. Garnet would have bet that Raven hadn't even told him about her — just wafted off somewhere and got on with it alone. Incapable of vowing *a year and a day, or however long your love should stay.*

At seven-thirty, Ebba's car hummed through the gates. Her car door banged. Garnet slummocked out to greet her. The new tenant had moved inside. A yellow strip of light glowed beneath his living room blinds.

Ebba lifted out books and folders and slammed the car door again. 'I saw a possum at the gate. Remember when we fed that little joey through the night?'

Garnet put her head to one side. 'I thought it would die.'

'We willed it to live. Lucky, *we* found it and not someone else.'

'Lucky not your daughter, you mean.'

'I didn't mean that, silly. Be nice.' Ebba glanced through the doorway at Raven, legs astride a small stool, weaving frame before her, threading in wild grass, lambswool gathered from barbed-wire fences, and tiny orchids plucked from the gullies.

As they came inside, Raven swayed slightly to the Celtic flute playing on the radio, and her fingers picked at the middle section of her design. Around her lay baskets of dried plants and flowers for the work, and at her feet an uncorked bottle. As they pushed past her into the kitchen she smiled.

'Ebba, do you know anything about the neighbour?' Garnet asked, gesturing outside.

Ebba grimaced. 'When I saw how close that cottage was to ours, I nearly didn't sign the contract, but the beauty all around just won me over.' She turned, threw her hands out from her belly to river and sighed. 'Short answer, no.'

Raven threw down a handful of native grasses and disappeared outside. Ebba tossed daisies into a sweet tomato salad with currants. Garnet picked at her food for a while, but when her mother didn't return, disappeared upstairs with a chunk of poppy-seed bread and fell asleep on her unmade bed. Later, she woke thick-headed and distracted and heard banging from the cottage yard next door.

Rolling onto her belly she peered through the window again. Guess who? Building something. Bare, muscled back leaning over to saw and lift wooden planks overhead, then hammering nails to join them to uprights.

Ting

Garnet swung her legs over the edge of the bed, crossed to the computer, and hit return to banish the screensaver. 'Gude spede.mov' from kimmer@paisley.net.uk appeared. She never opened strange attachments. *Oops.* It took an age to download.

Garnet liked to make clips for the others in which she read uplifting poems by Gerard Manly Hopkins in a dark voice or death-black poems by Wilfred Owen in a sweet voice, contorting her face like a madwoman. English teachers gave out Plath and Woolf like jellybeans and hoped senior students wouldn't kill themselves under pressure.

Repeat after me... do not open unknown files. The quality was poor, dark and grainy, and the film wouldn't maximise to full screen, but she clicked on the play arrow anyway. Clutching her throat, a white-faced girl, shawl drawn around her shoulders, panted through dense undergrowth. Dogs barked in the background. Voice muffled by wind; the girl cried out. Then fell in an untidy heap in front of a row of wooden crosses. Where was she — in a cemetery? Garnet aimed a spit of sugar free gum at the bin and decided to run the vid through again.

It had gone. A doomy worm? She would have to run a check. She trawled for the video in the trash, but not a sign remained. She searched the web for a trace. Nothing came up for kimmer@paisley.uk. How weird was that? The email had disappeared into cyberspace.

She wondered whether 'gude spede' was 'God speed' or 'good speed'? So kimmer — a loop from where? She hadn't accepted anyone called kimmer: a gossip, a 'gude' wife, according to the *Dictionary of Scots Language*. Not the same thing, surely?

Paisley, she knew. Paisley appeared in their family tree. Old Nana Miller came from Paisley, once a village in Scotland, now just a dreary suburb of Glasgow. Ebba's old Paisley shawl came from a local woollen mill. The email must have been a mistake.

Garnet glanced out the window and tried once more to concentrate on the *Crucible* girls, Abigail, Mercy, and Tituba with the ridiculous name, who had all danced, drunk blood and conjured up dead sisters. Tituba had been the Reverend's slave in Barbados. Go figure that, a Christian man. The play seemed way extreme, and she felt tired.

Ebba considered herself a country-dweller, looking to the entire natural world with reverence. Even plants in pots contained useful energy, she said, and should never be allowed to die. Garnet knew that her Nana was solitary, working in the garden, observing simple rituals, looking for harmony in her life. People were so stupid about things like that. Cody had asked her once if her family were witches.

'Why would you even ask?' Garnet answered. 'Ebba meditates, is all.'

'My mum thinks Ebba and Raven are weird. Not *you*.'

'I can't believe your mother would say that. She doesn't even know them.' A nugget of fear solidified in the pit of her stomach and Garnet glowered at Cody, who shrugged and backed right off.

'Forget it. I've got your back.'

Anyone living with Raven would crave harmony, Garnet knew. Knotting and un-knotting ribbons, lighting candles and chanting seemed to centre Ebba but, even so, town gossips would dump her with the dark practitioners that people read about or saw in movies. Ebba had counselled kids who were born into oddball-groups that made *do what you will but harm none* a mockery. She told Garnet that because someone had damaged their sense of self, the members of these groups went on to screw things up for other people.

Who wasn't damaged? It didn't have to be diabolical – just life. No one Garnet knew led a normal life: a TV life, where problems could be solved in sixty minutes, give or take an ad. But the *witch* word couldn't be taken lightly. Nor easily denied. *The Crucible*, for all its extremity, revealed how fear and guilt worked. Power ruled. People had died and it hadn't always been *little crazy children are the keys of the kingdom* — not at all.

She found Ebba in the bedroom. 'While I was reading *The Crucible*... A film message arrived by email from Paisley.'

Ebba looked up from her novel and nodded.

'It's where your mad lot came from — the previous owners of all that stuff in your time-warp museum – I mean, bedroom? Do we have witches in our family?'

Ebba looked sad. 'I think you're taking your school text too literally.'

'Eb, you can cold boot if you want but you're home now. No need to answer a question with a question and you can forget that para-phrasing crap.'

'Your Paisley great-great-great-grandfather's name was James Miller.'

'Arthur *Miller* wrote *The Crucible*.'

'Slow down, darling. No relation.'

'And what about my ancestor's woman?'

'Elisabeth McAlpine married James twice at Paisley Abbey in 1853, a year before they embarked with their children on a boat bound for South Australia.'

'Twice. That's extreme.'

'Perhaps because he was a church elder. Who knows. I don't'

Ebba picked up a silver frame on the bedside table to show Elisabeth and James picnicking on the banks of the River Cart, arms around each other's waist, their eyes scouring an ashen sky, as if searching for an answer.

Australia. Come to Australia, Garnet wanted to shout. She flumped on Ebba's bed and stretched out, hands clasped behind her head. Elisa-beth's hair looked long enough to sit on.

'James was a dowser, you know,' her grandmother said.

'Excuse me?'

'He could divine for water. It is a gift.'

'I knew we were a gifted family.'

'My Nana believed a twin brother built a boat at the slipway with James and set off for Australia. But he never arrived. Twins can be the worst kind of omen.'

'What is it with you and twins? The brother could have washed ashore in Africa.'

'Perhaps he never existed. Or he could be fish food at the bottom of the Indian Ocean.'

'Bleakness. Just asking because of the email.' Garnet threw her school polo shirt over her face and peddled her legs in the air.

Ebba pulled it down again. 'And what did it say?'

'Nothing. Film clip'.

'Yes, and?'

'Just a crazy woman running aboot.'

'Curious. It may not have been intended for you.'

'I thought of that.'

'Naturally. Do you clean that heavy metal in your belly button?' Ebba leaned away from her desk and poked Garnet's navel ring with her finger.

'Nana – my space.' Garnet waggled a finger. 'Crash out now, if you don't mind.'

'Does Paisley town have a website? I don't remember a huge amount about the place.'

Ebba had the Paisley thing bad. Her room was already full of tasteless family stuff: peacock feathers in a brass pot on the sill, for instance. Bad luck, Garnet knew that for a fact. Raven said inside, the feathers courted bad karma. And glass cabinets stuffed with old Miller china and bits and pieces that Ebba had collected overseas, like African ivories, a very big no-no — highlight and delete; leather camels; microscopic Jesus pictures from South America; Scotty-dog brass letter openers; and teacups with heather painted on them.

Ebba had also kept old Nana Miller's brown teapot, a porcelain Cavalier King Charles spaniel with a blue bow and a pansy face, scotch thistle short bread tins, and framed twin tapestry thingies. Had she been a twin too? Most of her stuff was crammed in glass cabinets because Ebba said dusting was an anachronism. Well, what about keeping all that junk? That had to be an anachronism, but whatever. Garnet liked her own friendly dust and drew pictures in it with her finger. She dusted her computer: usually with a pair of seasoned knickers scooped off the floor. No point in crapping up her hard drive.

But Garnet really liked the Paisley shawl that also appeared slung around Nana Miller's shoulders in her wedding photograph. French soldiers, Ebba told, had brought beautiful shawls back from Egypt during the world wars and they had become hugely fashionable. Paisley weavers had copied the pine symbol and mass-produced them. She had shown Garnet how to scrunch Nana's shawl just the right way into the little silk bag it lived in, so that it shook out fresh and full of colour, with no fold lines or faded bits.

Lately Ebba had taken to draping the shawl across her pillows. If she eventually lost her marbles, Garnet was sure she would want to go and live in Paisley – which could only be marginally better than living here, or in la-la-land with Raven.

Now the shawl rushed like a river of blood across the wooden Saratoga trunk at the end of the bed. The trunk had journeyed over the oceans from Paisley to a small town in Australia, where Millers had been the backbone of the Caledonian Society for years and years. Inside it lay sepia photos of uncles in kilts playing bagpipes, and aunties dancing the Highland Fling, Sword Dance and Sailor's Hornpipe. And maps and old Bibles, birth certificates, Raven's baby curls, and a complete baby layette. Seriously boring.

Garnet blew Ebba a kiss before she left the room, then skidded in her socks along the passage, on her way upstairs to lie on her bed. Her grandmother didn't trade much in kisses, but she had paid for a modem. Remarkable, from a woman who watched the direction of the wind, took care throwing out bones, and picked up hair, fingernails, sticks and stones, to prevent anyone using them against her.

Early on, when the bills came in, Garnet had kept a very low profile. But Ebba understood how much the computer helped with homework, and knew that girls liked being totally alone, and totally not. Online.

· · ·

The sky darkened. Garnet's slumped and weary body reflected in the window. A light bulb glowed behind her and damp-stains formed shapes on the walls. Did everyone feel incomplete? Or just only children? Shifting light and strange outlines in mirrors might not spook most girls. Shadows moved across the yard. Fog crept in to shroud the silver half-moon. The owl continued to cry out from the trees. *Boobook, boobook, boobook.* And the man next door hammered his wood.

Garnet flicked off her bedside lamp so he couldn't see her. Then she pushed into the window recess to watch him tack rolls of wire around a wooden construction which looked like a cage. Wooden perches — so birds, perhaps, not monkeys. How mad to stay up until almost midnight building a giant aviary with separate rooms. She supposed the birds were in the little crates he had unloaded earlier in the evening. Next, he swigged beer straight from a bottle. So nothing.

Ting

Cody: you asleep?

Garnet: Was. Nodded off reading *The Crucible*. Then I got a funny email.

Cody: say more.

Garnet: Film clip from kimmer@paisley.net.uk

Cody: Run that past me again.

Garnet: Nah. Someone stuffed up. I'm wacked.

Cody: Really?

Garnet: None of your business.

Cody: You think too much. Chill out.

Garnet: I do. How are you feeling?

Cody: Sure.

Garnet: Love you.

Cody: I hope something happens for *me* soon.

Garnet: Better not.

· · ·

Ting

Zane: hi.

Garnet: What's up?

Zane: Are you aware how many hacking sites exist?

Garnet: Are you trying to tell me something?

Zane: Do you have a problem sharing online with new friends?

Garnet: Absolutely.

Zane: the smugness of a closed mind.

Garnet: obsessive. Night.

Ting

Daisy: Hi.

Garnet: Hi.

Daisy: How many people run illegal software? In Australia?

Garnet: You been talking to Zane?

Daisy: It's pure anarchy out there. Zane is the new virus.

Garnet: Zane the mouth

Daisy: Zane the nose

Ting

Cody: what is with the black this week, Garnet? You going Goth?

Garnet: Sure. I brood. I emote. Go to sleep, you.

When Ebba's rooster crowed at midnight, the clock stopped dead and Garnet shivered. Risking one more peep out the window, she at first caught only her reflection, and the dissolving image of the small boy. A trick of the light. The moon shifted from behind black clouds and lit up the man standing beside the driveway, hands on hips, head thrown back in the chill breeze. Staring up at her. *Don't @ me, freak.*

Chapter Two

OVERCOMING EVIL

Ting

Cody: Might be late this morning. Wait for me. Madwoman alert. Mum came home from Zonta last night. Said the women caned Ebba and Raven again.

Garnet: Serious? I wish they'd get off their case. They might be weird but they don't pay people out like them good citizens. Go back to *The Crucible.* Remember page 100: *ipso facto* can't be proven until after the fact.

Cody: Little genius, I don't know what you're talking about. Reading books brought Giles Corey's wife to the gallows.

Garnet: More like he did. Ebba and Raven have done nothing to hurt the Zonta women. Says more about them, beating up *invisible crimes.* Why? I'll wait for you at the oval gate. xx

Cody really knew how to press her buttons. Who gave a flying fuck what people thought? If Ebba was out there sky-clad, scaring the cows off their milk, it'd be one thing, but even she admitted she was past it.

Freezing her tits off to get close to nature was a youthful thing — like when Garnet and Cody used to play Strip Jack Naked with Cody's brattish little brother, and they all ran down the Inman Road with their tops off. None of them would do it now. Ever.

Some townspeople yattered. Hard to miss them, bodies turned to block Raven out, eyes following her after she had passed. Probably prefer her mother got maggoted at the football club on Saturday night. Rather Ebba played games with the old blokes full of secrets at the Masonic Lodge. Rather anything, than let innocent women live their own lives. Raven only endangered herself. Ebba went to a few meetings in the city, pottered in her garden and was, in fact, totally harmless.

Once Raven had tried to put the wind up Garnet late at night, pointing down to Ebba, who was digging a circular bed near the oak tree. Garnet could only just make out her shape in the shadows by the river but could hear the thunk of the shovel and an occasional clink when it connected with stones. Then Ebba had dug something up and carried it on the spade in front of her across the yard to the burning bin. The neighbour's dog went bonkers. Raven leaned against Garnet, smoke from her joint trailing out the window.

'What's Ebby doing?'

Raven made a spooky face and hissed, 'Mandrake.'

Garnet opened her mouth in the spirit of enquiry, and closed it again. Afterwards, trying not to look too obvious, she looked up *mandrake*, a plant with white flowers, its roots shaped like a small human form. If you hit them with a spade they squealed. Sometimes it freaked Garnet out that Raven knew such things. Perhaps she had coveted one for her own garden and brought home a cutting. No doubt she picked up ideas on her enforced holidays with nut-jobs at the hospital. Mandrake could sedate and kill pain.

Ebba most likely had been burning the rubbish that blew in from the main road. Enjoying the wind-down after her long day in the city, she often worked at night. Raven demanded attention, 24/7. How could Garnet ever lead a normal life with a mother like her, who had left her with nothing shocking to do or say?

. . .

School had become terminally boring. Even or especially in the back row, Garnet felt stuck as she observed the team-sporty girls take themselves off to an interschool volleyball comp in the gym. After the match they returned to class making a hell of a racket. The relief teacher ran around the room trying to put out deliberately lit spot-fires, only to see another flare up, set by shrieky, sweaty overheated girls. Order broke down. In panic, the reliever picked on innocents, like Mick, reading Tolkien beside Garnet in the back row.

'Take your feet off the desk,' the reliever shouted at him.

Had Garnet not skipped two grades to take this class. For what? To shout 'rhubarb' into the rabble. Ahead of the curriculum in her own year level, she could at least withdraw and read. Hapless, Garnet raised her eyebrows at the teacher, turned it into a wicked sneering combo and received a grey card: Class Expulsion Notice. In sympathy, Lyndon placed three fingers to his forehead.

From the corridor into which Garnet had been expelled, she could hear Zane flirting with the teacher, who likely couldn't stand cocky boys. When the bell rang, the Year Twelves sloped off to the bus lines. Zane waited slouched up against the gym wall until she shuffled from the principal's office, paperwork in her satchel. Garnet scowled at him and passed without comment.

At home she inhaled a soy thick shake – stress made her hangry. Why not, after all, lift an essay on *The Crucible* from the hundreds of links, including the movie? 'The world has gone mad.' She nibbled at a few free articles, felt deep sorrow for the Salem girls. They had been as bored as her.

Unable to choose their clothes or speak unless spoken to, they were stuck on the edge of a wilderness full of wild animals and Red Indians — sorry, Native Americans — with no net access. Forced to spend hours at prayer and doing housework. Anyone would go nuts. A romp in the forest and a taste of power had made their day.

Two hundred people jailed, one of them four years old — Jumping Jesus! Just girls wanting to put their finger on the go button. Most days, Garnet felt like that. Cody, too, who couldn't wait to leave town.

Testimonies and petitions from descendants of witches who wanted memorials and official exonerations, flowed beneath her cursor. Could not blame them. Scene summaries bobbed up but no decent essays in the first thirty links at least. Garnet didn't want to pay, and her brain felt overloaded. Seeking consoling and consumable junk, she thumped downstairs to the kitchen, smacked her hand against a rope of garlic hanging from the mantelpiece. Why couldn't Ebba and Raven shop like normal people?

Ting

Pockets stuffed with dried nectarines and nuts, she took the stairs two at a time and slid in her socks across the landing to her room

Another kimmer file had arrived: 'nae word did she say – child wadna mend.mov'. Twice couldn't be an accident. When the clip opened, the same girl stood backed up against a stone wall, the same shawl round her shoulders. Not a Paisley shawl — Garnet knew immediately – no little tear-drop shapes in the pattern.

Strange black marks despoiled the girl's neck but looked more daubed on than bruising – could be from a paint program – and although her face was hidden by her dishevelled hair and raised hand, the girl looked stressed to the max. Mouth full of nuts, Garnet leaned forward. Same problem as last time. The frame wouldn't maximise or save. She tried back arrow to rewind – poof. Instantly, the film dissolved in pixels, like transitions between slides on a show, and disappeared from the screen.

No trace in the trash. Weirder and weirder. Who or what could kimmer be? Garnet felt a surge of something resembling excitement. She created a 'kimmer' folder on the desktop in which to drop notes.

Film 1: White-faced girl wearing a velvet bonnet and shawl runs, hand over her mouth. Scared or about to throw up? Dogs bark, she cries, falls in heap in front of a wooden cross.

Film 2: Same girl, scared witless, backed up against a wall as if she has no avenue of escape. Bruised neck. Had someone hit her?

. . .

Garnet lay on her bed and kicked her legs. When Ebba came home, she would ask her opinion. At Sappho, bullying was her specialty. What then, if she thought Garnet at risk and took back the computer? Proceed with care. The films must be a joke. So not funny. Some long-lost Paisley relatives had found out about the Australian Millers and wanted to play mean games. She nodded off.

Garnet woke hot and grumpy. Leaning dreamily out the window, she could see her grandmother picking oregano in the herb garden. Could be pizza coming up. The man's car sunned itself like a silver reptile beside the cottage wall. Garnet hauled on her boots and slipped out through the back door, where she found Ebba pouring milk into a shallow dish.

'I wish you wouldn't do that,' she grumbled.

'We can't desert our friends at the end of a hot, dry summer. We need to build them up before winter.'

'Why?' Garnet pouted. 'I hate snakes, and I don't like surprises at my back door, even if it is only my foot in a bowl of cold milk.'

'Stop your greetin',' Ebba replied.

'What's Raven doing?'

'She's by the river, gathering three-pronged reeds for her workshop with Indigenous weavers at the Coorong tomorrow.'

From the garden, Garnet watched her mother move towards the bridge, knife flashing in the fading sunlight as she waded through the reeds, dropping stalks into a large flat basket, then carrying it in the opposite direction, dragging a stick behind her as she followed the sagging fence line along the riverbank. The sun dipped and Garnet shivered. Through the window, she could see Ebba inside lighting taper candles. Eventually, using two fingers, her grandmother would extinguish each of them and light them all again.

Wood-fire blew in curls from their neighbour's chimney, making the garden reeky. Ebba had planted three or four rows of flowers around the main beds and up to the river gate. Big Red geraniums and nasturtiums splashed bold against the fence, and a few late red-hot pokers stood guard. Inside the red rows marched a border of yellow as a warning against the sun.

Dialogue from *The Crucible* had infiltrated her brain. '*This is a sharp time, now, a precise time – we live no longer in the dusky afternoon when evil mixed itself with good,*' she mumbled, '*and befuddled the world.*'

Amazing that some text stayed with her, even though exams were open book, and the rote-quote exam dead and buried. Memorising them must have been unconscious. She glanced uneasily at lengthening shadows along the riverbank.

At the edge of the rocky rapid part of the river, she sat, knees pulled up beneath her chin, drew shapes in the dust with a stick. The frantic-coloured sun rested on the western lip of the valley. The temperature had dropped. A chill breeze gathered up her skirt and whipped round her thighs.

She should talk to Lyndon more. Was he shy, or just quiet? Maybe he thought she was an idiot, getting kicked out of class like that. *Out of character.* And he'd be right. Only Zane loved to push teachers' buttons and called 'mayhem' his middle name. Zane's mother — stressed to the max and totally reactive — had become a single parent by default, with better-than-average resources. Hard to sympathise. But sometimes, trudging home after school, humping his heavy bag full of books and hardware, he looked quite miserable. He claimed that his father, a busy GP on-call 24/7, criticised and ignored him by turns.

A footfall crack between the trees forced Garnet's attention, and she swung her head as her heart quickened. If anything happened, Raven would never come looking for her – that was for sure. Something flashed between the low bushes at the river bend. Not binoculars.

She squinted into the lowering sun. Who would watch her out here? She jumped up and hurried home through the scrub. A great staring bovine thing would probably come crashing out. Cows were curious creatures and often surprised her. When they heard her in the back yard they often lined up along the fence, stared over, heads nodding, jaws moving rhythmically.

A pizza smell clarified in the air. The best distraction when she freaked out about *anything*. Soon, after the first rains, mushrooms would reappear on the menu. Ebba would fry them gently and stuff them into baguettes with grilled slices of Brie and chopped thyme. Garnet rushed to wash her hands.

After dinner, she borrowed Ebba's shawl and sat hunched in front of her monitor as she searched Paisley sites. She zipped around Wiki. How had people found things out in the olden days – pre-search engine? Waited three weeks for an inter-library loan. Life must have been so dull and slow. Ebba said old Nana Miller had been kirked in her Paisley shawl at Paisley Abbey. *Kirk* was the Scottish word for church. Garnet knew that, but she hadn't known that the Paisley Harness Plaid had been a universal bridal present or that Queen Victoria had bought half a dozen for her son's christening. By then, though, the industry had been in trouble.

Garnet stuck her head over the banisters and yelled. 'Ebba. Do we still have family in Paisley?'

'I have a great-aunt who occasionally writes to me.'

'Any kids?'

'Not heard of any. Why?'

'Just curious.' The kimmer e-mail definitely came from the UK and from a service provider named Paisley. The clips looked old, but they couldn't be. Could they? The girl's movements were indistinct and kind of jerky.

Garnet swirled the shawl around her shoulders in front of her reflection and watched two shawls settle on two sets of shoulders. She was seeing double again. Must be schizophrenic. Or should she get her eyes checked? At least when the boy appeared, he hadn't commanded her to do evil. Perhaps she had a gift — second sight — and Nana Miller spoke to her via e-mail attachments. Ghosts were getting sophisticated — sending ripples from another century through ADSL phone lines. 'Heap of crap, Garn', she admonished herself. 'Settle.'

Out of the corner of her eye, she watched the door handle silently turn on its spindle, and Raven drift in, hair slicked back, eyes puffy and dreamy. Dirt tracked across her cheeks. Crying again. Garnet smelled something sweet. Breathless, her mother plucked the shawl from Garnet's shoulders, floated it out behind her like a matador's cape, then draped it over the mirror.

'Cover the mirrors, daughter. I've brought you raspberry tea.'

'Ebba won't like it if you get that stinky smell on her shawl.'

'Any homework?'

'I bet *you* never did any.'

Raven looked pensive. 'I wasted opportunities. I want things to be different for you.'

Garnet placed her pillow over her face as if to blot out her mother's presence. Mothers were supposed to have their act together. When she looked up next the room was empty. She was sick of Raven's moodiness. A faint smell lingered. Gamey. Rank.

Chapter Three

WATER: PROTECTION

The river had always been Garnet's favourite place to think, and now the man had spoiled it. In the early morning, she heard him creak open the doors of cages, speak to the birds in his low refined voice. Now she would never be alone again.

He tossed handfuls of grain onto the cage floors. Some of the birds looked like racing pigeons. They made curdling noises at all hours. At five o'clock, when he let them out, they darted back and forth between the trees, up the hillside and back. When he called them down, their tagged feet clattered on the iron roof. Within days, a pair of peregrines from the waterfall saw this activity as a dinner date. Overhead, they circled the cottages, beaks arrowed down for the kill. Had acute hearing cued them in? Perched on the granite walls above the waterfalls, protecting their nests and chicks, they always warned her off. *Caccccarcc-ccarccccarack'*

Garnet had run two k's to the dairy and back, for the sheer hell of it, nicked a chunk of herb bread from the kitchen, and then mooched hot and sweaty down to the river. How annoying to find him, his long black-clad legs dangling in the water, at her place by the bridge. Even worse, he patted the stone next to him and looked up to greet her. Head down, she attempted to slide past without eye contact.

'Do you like yabbies?' he called out.

'We don't like to eat them. We're vegetarian. Mostly.' She turned her head towards home.

'Then I supposed roast squab pigeon must also be out of the equation.' He jumped up and held out his hand to her. 'My name is Branwell.'

From a standoffish distance she leaned in to shake and noted that his eyebrows met across his nose. Meh! 'Garnet,' she mumbled, wishing that she could avoid touching his hand. Her fingers leapt away. Aware her socks had fallen to her ankles and her running shoes were filthy, she leaned away poised to go.

'Stay and tell me about yourself.' He held out his hand as if to stay her.

Another one of those men who gave instructions. Like a teacher. *You need to...* blah, blah. *Be more specific about what you mean*, blah, blah.

Her eyes shied away. Dead giveaway that she'd taken offence.

'Do you like birds?' His voice stayed even.

'Not in cages.'

'I let them fly out at dusk. Have you noticed?'

'The peregrines will kill them.'

'Natural, I suppose.'

'Even though they're small, peregrines dive-bomb at vicious speed,' she said, irritated. 'They snatch baby rabbits and other birds and tear them to pieces.'

'Don't worry, I have them in my sights, and I have a gun.' She wished he hadn't said that. And then he smiled, which made him look charming, but she wasn't sure about him. 'Do you know a lot about birds...?'

Her indrawn breath felt almost imperceptible, even to her. Her focus shifted to trails of blue binder twine tied to the barbed wire fence and to the rubbishy river slurry. Was he staring back at her?

'Not really. The peregrines belong here.' She wanted to say, *you don't*, but that was mean. 'Will you stay at the cottage often?' she ventured in dread.

'I have a lot of work to do, and my wife has been quite ill.' Ravelling up the rope, he swung the net onto the bank and lifted out four yabbies with his long slim fingers. They flailed their legs when he held them from behind, dropped them in his bucket, and snapped down the lid.

'I'm sorry,' she said. 'I need to go.'

He squatted near the net to replace his bait and then stood up to swing the basket back into the water.

'You can take some yabbies with you if you like.' He stretched up beside her and smiled at her. Apart from the monobrow, she supposed he was good-looking.

'Thank you.' She pulled away, her feet awkward, wrong-footed. 'But better not. My mother will have already cooked dinner.'

Garnet sought Ebba in the glassed-in sunroom at the back of the cottage, where she was reading with a bowl of elderberry oatmeal in her lap, and curled up on the couch beside her. Ebba put her spoon down to pat her leg. 'All good, in your world?'

'I suppose. What do you think about the new neighbour?'

'Oh him. Nothing to report. Close to zero data.'

'Fair.'

Garnet closed her eyes. Mr Renshaw had a wife. That could be good. He might keep away from Raven. If the peregrines killed his pigeons, it wouldn't be her fault. She wondered what was wrong with his wife. Perhaps Ebba would ask him. Raven, probably not.

Soon enough, she forgot about him and began to think about the Paisley messages again. She crept down the passage with a mug of Milo and a chunk of fruitcake. Ebba knew better than to tell her she'd ruin her appetite; Garnet was never sure what would be on offer for dinner, anyway. It might be one of Raven's weird recipes tonight. She tried not to worry that she'd misled the man about gifting the yabbies.

She tapped lightly at her keyboard, munching cake, pushing hair from her face with the back of her hand. She wondered what Cody and the others were doing. The computer burred softly in the dark.

Garnet loved to imagine the structure of the web. It was such a mass of complex interactions, just like a cobweb, all the lines mysteriously secreted all over the world. Nothing existed permanently in cyberspace;

everything was in transit. Lines not maintained fell away and others intersected uncritically. The randomness and beauty of it took her breath away.

And now she could paint a picture in her head of old Paisley, where Marjorie, daughter of Robert the Bruce, died giving birth to a child who took the Scottish throne and founded the line of Stewart kings. And of Paisley Abbey where Elisabeth McAlpine, great-great grandmother of Ebba, great-great-great-grandmother of Raven, great-great-great-great-grandmother of Garnet, shivered in her Paisley shawl, before she took vows that would lead her across the sea to Australia.

Garnet scrolled through history, checking and crosschecking sites, and reading stories about artisans who worked with lawns and silks and muslins, who sang, wrote poetry, and bred birds. Were there Millers among them? Breeding birds bothered her when they could do it perfectly well by themselves. Unless they were rare and threatened species. She slid from link to link, noting names and places. She printed out maps and ran her pen along the cobbled streets, underlining Sma Shott's cottage and Shuttle Street, looking for Millers and McAlpines in the ship building yards of the Rivers Cart and Clyde.

Did her family build dredgers, blend fine malt whiskey, create litany, thread or golden-shred marmalade? Why did James and Elisabeth leave Paisley? There was so much she didn't know. Maybe Ebba could write and ask her great-aunt some questions. Would she have the answers?

In her hunt for family connections, she stumbled across a 1697 Paisley witchcraft story about a young 'girle' named Christian Shaw, who, having 'lange been ill', began to fit and vomit feathers, bones, eggshells, hair and lumps of shite. Well done her. She raved and swooned and threw herself around the room. When it came to the attention of her local ministers, they prayed and counselled her. She spouted Bible text. She levitated. She lay catatonic upon the floor.

Her parents were appalled. As anyone would be. Thirty-seven links included Amazing Facts on Paisley, Children as Accusers, Paisley Facts, and A Psychiatric Assessment_: *Scottish Medical Journal :41*.

According to David Drakon, her English teacher, the 1642 witch-hunt in Salem, retold in *The Crucible,* had come well after European witch-hunts, but the Paisley hunt had played out even later. Perhaps she could lift a quote for her essay. Garnet read through dinnertime.

'Yes,' she called down the stairs. 'I'm coming. In ten minutes. Stay calm.' She stayed in front of the screen.

Christian Shaw's appalling tale ended at the gallows on Paisley Green. Eleven people she accused of hexing her had been arrested and imprisoned in Paisley Tollbooth, with seven found guilty of witchcraft, and six of them executed. Garnet copied and pasted and dragged images into new folders.

If only she had paid better attention in class. That morning Drako had raved on and on about the European witch-hunts. Garnet vaguely recalled that their trials connected with the Reformation: something to do with Catholics and Protestants using the idea of witches to distract people from the main game of drumming up numbers for their churches.

Preoccupied, then, with a more pressing back-row pleasure, giving in to the temptation to tickling each other's legs like they used to, and Garnet had only caught snippets of that lesson. Cody's delicious feather-touches made titillating sweeps toward Garnet's knicker-line. Her fingers curled beneath the hem. Garnet had hunched over her desk, legs splayed, eyes glazed over, while Drako's voice vibrated like a distant fly. They were too old to get away with it much longer, even in the back row. It was not unheard-of for teachers to advance rapidly up the aisle and crash a metre ruler down on student desktops. And so, he did.

'What are you doing?'

'We're listening.' Bunched over, Garnet tried to fly below his radar. Alternative responses sprang to mind: *filing my nails, expressing pus from my new piercing, writing malicious notes, studying salacious pornography,* or even *licking my desk.* Why couldn't Drako keep their attention? In all sincerity, she found the subject interesting. Perhaps it was all about his tone. Maybe she could ask Lyndon about the play later. He'd probably studied it when he was in Year Ten.

Homework often made Garnet feel tired and depressed, but how serendipitous of Drako to set *The Crucible*, which might help her come to grips with family history in Paisley and her weird emails. While she had confided about the possible family witchcraft connection to Cody, no one else knew her family was from Paisley, or about the witch drama there. If she had mentioned the surprising film clip to Zane or Lyndon or even Daisy in passing, she had no recollection of it. Laying her head on the keyboard she heard Raven calling her from downstairs and she turned down the volume of her music.

'I'm coming!'

Raven lay full-length along the couch, a small towel pressed against her forehead. Peppermint oil warmed in a burner beside her.

'Mother, did you know that Scottish folk regard green as a magic colour, but feared putting it in their stomachs because it might contain arsenic?' Garnet began. 'Think of the bairns licking the wallpaper until their faces turned pale, their hands and feet icy cold, their stomachs going into spasm and their body expelling everything.'

'Don't be gruesome when I have a migraine. Ebba has gone to a meeting. Please go next door and ask for a Panadol.'

'Why can't *you*?'

'Darling, I'm ill.' Raven raised her arms in helpless surrender. Silver bangles cascaded down her arms and hoopla'd at her wrist.

Of course, she did vomit sometimes with migraines, but why should Garnet go? What would Raven have done if the cottage had still been empty? Garnet thought about refusing, but if she didn't agree, Raven would look wan and pale and reproachful all night, which would make downloading and playing loud music out of the question later. In either case, it would be painful.

'I don't really like him, Raven.' Garnet bit her lip. 'Did you know the Scots buried suicides at crossroads?'

'For God's sake, I'm not asking you to start a relationship with him. Just go to his door and ask for a few painkillers. You'll have to learn to deal with men sometime.'

'All right but remember that daily I'm dealing with unformed males, at their least evolved. You're not out there, Raven.'

Garnet slammed the flyscreen door and crossed the yard to the door of the second cottage. A pair of mud-encrusted boots stood beside her on the step. As she waited, she peered through a leadlight panel and saw *him* bare-chested, seated at a little table, tearing at food that had probably once been alive. Gloomy music droned through the walls.

'*I see no light of God in that man,*' she parroted. If he were *completely* naked when he stood up, she would drag the hose to the door. But when he answered the door, he had tied a large bath towel at the hip. He was holding the blackened leg or tail of a small creature and waggled it at her.

How did one avoid looking at men's bumps? Adult males had no shame, and boys' Speedos were the grossest torture. How could they not be embarrassed? Why did they not carry manbags and place them, strategically, at all times? Feeling red and stupid and miserable, she stared down at her feet.

'Garnet.' He lingered over her name. Seemed to caress it. 'Please excuse me. I worked out, and have just taken a shower.' In a room stacked with black and chrome gym equipment and fuggy with men's B.O., she could that see he was probably telling the truth. So, he was a gym-junkie, too.

He waved her in and slid back into his seat at the table. Continued eating. So rude.

'River-duckling legs are excellent.' He quirked an eyebrow. 'I'm saving the muddy crustaceans for tomorrow night.'

Garnet hated games. 'Raven has a migraine. She wondered if you have any Panadol.'

Dabbing at his mouth with a serviette he pushed the bowl aside. 'Indeed. I may have something stronger.'

She shrugged. Her mother would love that. He had rows of bottles packed into cardboard boxes stacked up in a corner of the room. He upended one, spilled a handful of small, yellow pills into a plastic zip-top bag, and moved toward her.

When she held out her hand, he dropped the snap lock bag onto her palm, turned her hand, and smoothed his fingers around it. Swiftly Garnet withdrew her hand and moved towards the door, taking great care not to dislodge the rifle upright against the wall. Gaia — a gun! He smiled, revealing his perfect teeth.

The night had turned black — no moon, no stars. As she stumbled toward her own back door, she could hear the soft chug of a sprinkler on the camomile lawn. A sixth sense caused her to hesitate near the door. A shimmering thing lightly uncoiled by her feet. The snake's head reared up, wavered and dipped, and then slid away. Amazing that she had noticed anything at all, and hadn't plonked her foot right down on top of it.

Bloody Ebba, whose car engine now growled at the front gate. Home from her meeting. Garnet waited to pay her out, as she helped carry in sheaves of papers, books and boxes.

'I just had a close encounter of the reptile kind. I wish you wouldn't feed them.'

Ebba shrugged. 'You're not worried about them, are you?' She squeezed her waist. 'Snake, or lizard?'

'Snake, and I'm not *worried*, but they make me feel funny. I don't especially like surprises.'

'Are you sure...? Not a sleepy lizard?'

'Oh, *sure.*'

'What are you doing out here?'

'Reclaiming the night. No, I'm joking. I've been next door cadging drugs for your daughter. That guy makes my skin crawl.'

Ebba touched her hair. 'Listen to your feelings and remember that ethics are more important than sins.'

'Unfortunately, I have no idea what you're talking about.'

'Never mind, darling. You will one day. What have you been doing?'

'Nothing much. Reading about Paisley. Have you heard of Christian Shaw?'

'Well yes, I vaguely remember the story — strange. I believe that after all those people were hung, she resumed a normal life, grew up, became a fine spinner and a weaver, and ran a most successful business. Married late. I suspect her story scared her suitors. If they didn't treat her right, she might have accused them.'

'I wouldn't rush to marry her.'

'At the age of twenty-nine, she married the local Reverend Miller. Brave soul.'

'A Miller. I haven't read that part yet. Could we be related?'

'Possibly or unlikely.'

'Ebba, there could be a link.'

'Well, there could be. But I don't know of it.'

'Why do I bother with the net when my own granny is such a font of knowledge? Ah, but I can't resist. I'm addicted. I'll call out to you if I find something important.' Garnet tossed the plastic pack of pills into her mother's lap and flew up the stairs.

Ebba called after her. 'Don't stay up too late.'

'Don't stress. It's the weekend, remember.'

Ting

Lyndon: I thought of you with hair in your face.

Deeply strange. He had attached a .wav file titled 'Silence'. It had better not be one big silence. She loaded the song and lolled back in her chair. But the music was nice, Gothic, and suited her mood. She let it wash over her, waved her hands over her head, and beckoned to the spider sitting like a fat full stop on the top of her cupboard.

Garnet: I'm tripping on the English moors. Fog's rolling in. Stay way cool.

Ting

Cody: The weekend is deadly, dark and doomed. Nana's dying. Leaving for Adelaide. Catchya, Codes.
Garnet: I'm sorry about your nana.
Cody: TTYL

Ting

Zane: my old man seems more than mildly curious about our relationship.
Garnet: we're not having a relationship.
Zane: Sorry. How's your mother? I found her medical notes in

Dad's study. Two years ago, he treated her for... Can't spill that sort of stuff, on a need-to-know basis. Hey, but we could get together?

Garnet: You're a spoilt little shit and you're way out of order. Don't mess with my mother. Loser.

Zane: okay. What are you reading? Maybe I already know.

What did he mean by that? Garnet sectioned her hair, plaited all the pieces and rolled them into knots fastened with coloured pins, then snapped a pair of silver frog hair clips on either side of her part. Not bad for a nature-lover. She tried to forget about Zane and decided to defrag and speed up her computer... Later. Right now she wanted to get back to Paisley sites.

Good old Ebba. Christian Shaw *had* married a Reverend John Miller. Garnet searched for her children. Why would she want to be related to such a horrible cow? Just curious. Came from having a tidy mind. But no luck. John Miller seemed to have died soon after the wedding. Suspicious? Perhaps, in some clever way, Christian had killed him, before she went on to become incredibly famous as the brains of Bargarran Thread and travelled the continent to bring back new technology for her factory.

Christian must have been mad and she should have been depressed. All those people hung because of her. But then, during the first trial, she had been only ten or eleven, and people had believed her.

If she got off on power, why had she stopped accusing people? Garnet vaguely remembered Drako saying — for just a mega-second she must have tuned in — that witches were not generally executed in England, and that they usually got off with a warning.

Apparently not in Scotland. What a rude shock, to go to Gallow Green and watch. Something else she remembered from Drako's lesson. The whole community turned out for hangings and burnings. Jugglers, sideshows, sweet meats and hot pies added to the carnival atmosphere.

In Christian's case, the mob mostly blamed Katherine Campbell, her mother's servant, for bewitching the girl. The same woman had probably brushed her hair, served her nursery tea, sung songs to her, possibly even suckled her. How terrible, to put your nanny to death.

Garnet found forty sites on the Bargarran witch trials, and the Shaw family estate. She emailed a professor at Edinburgh University, an expert, who was chairing a symposium on the supernatural in medieval Scotland, and used the conference registration email address to ask him about the best book to read on the topic.

Ting
    Zane: Hello again
    Zane: I know you're there.
    Zane: I know what you're doing

Garnet draped a pair of black knickers over the camera on top of her computer and jumped into bed.

Chapter Four

PERSUASION: MEMORY

She woke feeling as hot as hell. The computer emitted a soft burr. The room smelled of plastic and active radiation.

Ebba materialised in the doorway.

'Have you slept in your clothes again? Your room looks like Afghanistan. And it's late. I bet you didn't even brush your teeth last night.'

It was almost midday, and Garnet still felt wrecked.

Branwell Renshaw's yellow pills must have kicked in, because Raven had left hours before for the Coorong. Ebba ordered Garnet to the shower, and then to the orchard and the dairy, for fruit and milk — *do not pass go; do not collect two hundred dollars*. Alright. No biggie. She would run there and walk back not to spill the milk. Running made her feel full-blooded, alive, *normal*, not like Raven.

On the way out, she said goodbye to Ebba, pegging washing on the line. No audible reply came through the mouthful of pegs.

At the orchard, the summer fruit had already been sold. A week or two ago, trays of nectarines, peacharines and gooseberries had sat outside the front gate on a table. Now they were back to boring old apples and pears. She bit into a nashi pear, probably last year's from the cool room, eased the paper bags of fruit into her backpack and slipped a few notes and some coins into the honesty box. Ebba thought the orchard fruit cheap and local, but remained unconvinced that the produce was organic.

'You want them coddly, do ya?' old Mrs McFarlane had said in a friendly way when Ebba complained about their perfection.

She'd walked down from the house when she noticed Garnet.

'Got a big weekend planned?' she asked. Mrs McFarlane was nice. Her kids had all left home. Left the country, in fact.

'I wish.'

'Never much to do in town...? At least you can go to the pictures, and I've heard you can hop around at the pub until midnight even if you're underage.'

'Raven and Ebba aren't too excited about me doing that. I go sometimes when I sleep over at Cody's. The music's dodgy though.' Garnet held out her container while Mrs M poured the milk and clipped on the lid. Fresh, warm and smelly, it came straight from the cows. She waved goodbye and set off home along the road.

At the first bend, a car roared up behind her, spitting dust and gravel around her feet. Garnet moved rapidly aside. Zane and Lyndon hung out the windows, looking pleased with themselves.

'What are you doing out here?' She eased her bags to the ground.

'Cruisin', Red Riding Hood. Want to bring your goodies for a ride in my car?'

'Not much.' She laughed. 'Where did you get that heap of shit?'

'The old man kept it in the shed. Lyndon's been giving me a hand doing it up.'

'Thanks for "Silence", Lyndon. I love it.' Garnet said, and noted his half-smile.

Zane moved closer. 'Come down to the river and have a fag.'

'I don't, remember? Anyway, the milk will go off.' She swung the billy, sloshing milk around.

'Been to the bush supermarket?' Lyndon grinned. 'You can always put the billy in the river to keep it cool.' The car continued to crawl along beside her.

'Hey, alright, I'll come for five minutes,' she said, making a show of giving in. Anything would be better than them following her home. The boys pulled over and got out, and the three of them scrambled down the riverbank where it overlooked an old wooden bridge.

'Any more clips from Paisley?' Zane asked. He was wearing cargo shorts, a baggy surf shirt and running shoes. Was he staring at her breasts?

'I didn't tell *you*, did I?'

'Cody told me.'

'I don't know why she bothered. It's nothing.'

Zane and Lyndon smoked. Garnet lay on her back between them until Lyndon stubbed his cigarette out and climbed up the riverbank to the car. As if on cue, Zane rose up on an elbow and leaned over her face, to outline her lips with a piece of dry grass.

So how come she didn't get to choose the moment or the boy? She and Cody often saw Zane with girls, walking up and down the main street on Saturday nights. Once, near the back of the Westpac bank, Zane had slung an arm around Garnet's shoulders and dipped his face into hers. She had shivered. Bodies betray people. She had made absolutely no decision about him, and yet, here she was again, warm and damp and soft inside, her heart beating fast. Why? Because he touched her skin?

'Where do you live? Nearby?'

'No. I'm just out walking on the wind.'

'Liar. I'll find out. Perhaps I already have.' He slid his finger under the hem of her crop top and made soft circles.

So good, but ... What if Lyndon came back? Why should Zane just change the temperature of their relationship without any consultation? But guys did, didn't they? Garnet sat up. Scrambled to her feet. Brushed down her clothes and gathered up her shopping.

Authority. How to get more? She remembered, then, about Raven.

'I've been thinking about what you said about my mother. Why would your father keep her notes at home?'

'Not a paper-free office. Clearly.'

'And...'

'Lots of reasons. Could be a letter of referral to a specialist.'

'You know, don't you? How dare he leave things around where you can read them?'

'It's me that does the daring.' Zane grinned, rose and swung away. 'Catch ya.'

Garnet felt glad when they roared away. It would have been a hassle to get rid of them before her turnoff. Although Zane could easily find out where she lived — likely already had, from her mother's file, if he hadn't already heard in passing. Living along the river made everything harder. Everyone in town knew where everyone else lived. They dropped in, hung around; came over; whizzed past on bikes and, when they turned sixteen, parked out the front or burned past. Garnet knew the town students thought her weird – like the rest of her family.

The afternoon rushed by, and early evening too, as Garnet moved from site to site, reading about the Scottish brand of witchcraft, cutting and pasting into files, hoping to clarify her thinking. She was glad she didn't live during those times, when most people in Europe were poor and looking for someone to blame.

When arguments flared up about tools and food, money and utensils, solitary women could be blamed more easily than foreign enemies. Epidemics, diseases or bad weather brought denunciations. Elders argued for killing *witches*, not *women*. It reminded her of news clips showing Afghani women begging on the streets, then being taken to a football oval and shot in the head. No wonder Christian Shaw and the girls in *The Crucible* seized their moment. Witchcraft was complex. But maybe a feminist thing? Necessary.

Abigail in *The Crucible* waited until she left her employer's house to accuse his wife. That way she could get back at him and not be punished. Perhaps Christian Shaw had been vindictive too. Perhaps she had been cooped up inside over a long winter and felt annoyed with the servant about something. Sometimes people accused others to get rid of them. She would kill two birds with one stone, putting Christian Shaw in context as she wrote her essay on Arthur Miller's play.

'Garnet. What are you doing?' called Ebba from the stairs.

'Studying.'

'Camomile? Help you think.' She passed a mug over the banisters.

Raven arrived home and deposited in the hallway armloads of rushes brought from the car. Quietness descended.

'Where is Raven now?' Garnet asked.

'Out walking. Not sure. She's a grown-up.'

'I didn't hear the car go.'

'No.'

Prone crone. On the couch. Ebba closed her eyes. Garnet stooped to kiss her.

Ting

Zane: Come out. Come down the street. I'll. Come. And get you.

Garnet: Fuckwit. I'm studying.

Zane: It's Saturday night. Semester 1.

Garnet: See you later.

Zane: Face 2 Face?

Garnet: N

An email arrived from the professor in Edinburgh. He believed that the Paisley trials and others in Scotland were linked to the actions of small local courts without direct oversight. Much like the religious nuts in Salem, Garnet thought. But Scottish women owned property, and men must have decided there was no other way to get it off them. No excuse. Wicked.

The professor had recommended a few books by Christina Larner. Garnet searched for her work online and finally found something in an academic bookshop with a web shop. She clicked the link and put in her address, borrowing Ebba's credit card to pay for it.

Her mind kept circling back. How could Christian Shaw have lived in that community after causing death in at least seven families? How they must have hated her. *Just a child*. Garnet bet her parents kept her away from the public until things settled down. But had *they* manipulated *her*?

She debated the relative merits of being the accuser and the accused. Perhaps Raven, angry with Ebba, really had planted her pair of elder trees to keep witches out. Garnet's head thickened with questions. Fuggy and overtired, she lay on her bed fully clothed. Who had slipped the lavender sachet beneath her pillow? Darling Ebba?

At midnight a chill night wind crept in the open window and, as she dipped in and out of sleep, Garnet tightened the feather quilt around her shoulders. A nightmare gripped her. Something amorphous but perhaps malevolent hovered over her bed. Fleeting images of Ebba astride a hare danced before her eyes. The pale detached face of mirror boy appeared. Images, not memories. A heavy weight crushed air from Garnet's chest and her brain struggled to command her arms and legs. Dreaming?

Outside, a horse galloped on the rising wind, birds rattled skywards, and the Paisley shawl slid suddenly from her mirror, and crumpled onto the floor with a *whoosh*.

A moon sliver cast just enough light on the yard to illuminate Raven flying light-footed towards the river, and someone loping along behind her — someone in tight black clothing, who looked strong and light on their feet. Garnet's lips tried to shape the word *Mother*. Raven backed up against a poplar, her flimsy clothing flapping round her legs. Her pursuer knelt now at her feet, half rose to run outstretched hands, from her ankles to her waist. Raven threw back her hair, shook it in the wind. Then broke away and ran again. The figure followed.

Garnet thought about spiders and the question of who lured whom. Felt a frisson of excitement as behind the trees her mother crouched and pulled the person down on top of her. The river glinted bright. Her mother's dress fluttered.

Who had decided on this course of action — the Branwell Man or Raven Mad? Was her mother calling out, 'I can't get involved with you. I hardly know you.' And would he reply, 'That's a shame,' before he devoured her pale face?

Switching on her lamp to dispel Gaia knew what, Garnet sat up and drank a glass of water from the bedside table. Swinging her legs over the side of the bed, she pulled the shawl off the mirror, and wrapped it around her shoulders, crept downstairs, and slipped into her mother's empty bed. She would wait for her. When she had been little, it had always worked to dispel her fears. But the sheets were still warm with a sweet smoky smell. Bad cess. This wouldn't do. She tiptoed back along the passage to her grandmother's room, where a thin line lit the doorway.

'Raven's out there, Ebba,' she whispered as she entered.

'Yes. I hope she's taking care.'

'What are you doing?'

'I'm working in bed. Here, eat some cake.' Ebba broke off a piece from the slice on the plate balanced on the covers and placed it her hand. 'I've warmed mead on the gas if you want some.'

Garnet very much liked honey mead. Returning with an earthenware mug, she felt the warmth chase through her body as she sipped. 'Are you chanting?'

'Yes.'

'To the goddess?'

'If you like.'

'For Raven?'

'For all of us.'

Ebba patted Garnet's cheek. 'Head back to bed now, there's a good girl.'

'How about a story?'

'And how old are you?'

Garnet faked a pout. 'Tell about Christian Shaw, Ebba. What if we are related? Would we be responsible for all those people she killed?'

'Think about official apologies.'

'You mean the Sorry thing? About not apologising to Indigenous people?'

'Yes, I suppose.'

'Mmm.' Garnet, Ebba and Raven agreed about that. *Sorry* was not enough, but even that still seemed to stick in the government's throat.

'You know that one of the Paisley accused never made it to Gallows Green,' Ebba said. 'He committed suicide in prison.'

Garnet sighed. 'The sites I visited just said he died.'

'By his own hand. I've been reading again too. After the first accusations, they lifted a mysterious horseshoe from the grave at the green. Fear rippled through the community. Then a textile worker, John Reid, hung himself.'

Garnet shuddered and pulled the shawl higher around her shoulders. 'The whole thing is gross. What if no one bewitched anyone? And all that evil came from the accusations.'

'It's not about truth, but power. But I don't think that it was our branch of the Millers that were responsible. As far as I know the Reverend Miller and Christian Shaw had no children.'

'We can't know for sure, though. How many Millers lived in Paisley then?'

'It must have been a common name in Scotland and in England. Think of all the mill keepers. I doubt we'll ever know our entire family line.'

'Oh, doom and rats.'

'Research all you want. Have I shown you these photos?' Ebba climbed out of bed and pushed up the lid of the trunk, taking care with the loose hinges, before she drew out a box of photographs. 'Look at this bonny man with his dress coat and dangling seals.'

Garnet fingered the photo. It was sepia, but in places had been tinted pink. 'He had nice skin. No beard?'

'Clean-shaven was the fashion then.' Ebba looked sad. 'Small communities are good places, unless you're different.'

'Ebba, you're a legend. I had a nightmare, but I think I can sleep now. Can you?'

'Things continue to improve at work. I channel my spiritual energies to resolve tension.'

'Speak English. You're not at work now.' Garnet sighed. '*Witch* is a way harsh word.'

'Words entrap. Even the word Wicca is masculine in essence.'

'You don't still go to meetings, do you?'

'Odd get-togethers in pubs. I miss the dance, Garnet. Dancing fills me with longing. It's not the same alone.'

'Dancing is dead sexy. What about sex?'

'People need to get in touch with all their selves, and "sexy" is one of them.' Ebba winked. 'Now off to bed.'

Garnet danced upstairs, humming a Foo Fighter song, shaking her yoni. She re-draped the wayward Paisley shawl over the cheval mirror, then decisively pulled down her window blind. She would not look. Her mother could go to the devil if she wanted.

Chapter Five

HOUSEHOLD: PROTECTING ANIMALS

Cody and Garnet had been training for school sports day. It was the only normal thing the school could reliably expect of them. The sports teacher thought Garnet ran for the school, but really, she ran for joy. Sweaty, not geeky. Running felt powerful. Strong. In control. Pushing off from the earth and falling back; legs obedient. Afterwards, she felt good — tired, but inexplicably good. She rolled up her sports clothes in a calico bag and ran through the gathering dusk to the bus stop. Thought happy thoughts all the way home.

Great. Someone had placed a pattern of stones on her front doorstep. Key in hand, she moved closer. YES, they spelled. Bloody Raven. YES. Garnet kicked them viciously. She glanced over her shoulder. Was he home? Paws crossed, his dog lay at the entrance to his kennel, something dangling from his sloppy jaws. After she identified it as a moor hen, she gagged and ran through the lavender, between the pairs of poplars, and down to the river. She gulped air. Gross, disgusting, too confronting. Focused on the glittering surface of the slowly moving water she reneged, so much for happy. Were dogs natural carnivores?

The pepper trees had flowered. Tiny sprays of the palest yellow isotopes frothed between the swaying leaves. She rushed past daphne forming tiny buds, and oleanders, those brassy-pink blooms that could poison stock. Ebba had made Raven chop them back. Foxgloves swayed beneath a pair of catkins. Damn. Raven must have inhaled before she planted half these things. All of them poison. Garnet pounded over the silver grass drying along the river's edge. *Bloody, bloody!* Why couldn't she have a normal mother, like Cody's? She leapt a rotting log, crunched through bark behind the willow tree and cannoned straight into *him*.

He reached out for her immediately as though to steady her, and then gathered her in, held her against his chest, his face too close to hers.

'I thought you were your mother,' he said.

As if Raven would crash about like she did. His voice sounded soft. It unnerved her. He held her with his eyes. Inexplicably, he leaned into her face, touched his lips to hers and then bit her bottom lip.

'You are an old man,' she snapped, pulling hard away from him.

'An old man who means no harm,' he said.

No harm! Tears welled. Her mouth hurt. Garnet ducked her head, knowing that soft streamers of willow leaves hid them from the house. In any case, everyone else was out. When he reached over and began to move his hands over her clothing, she erupted, threw herself backwards, finally broke free and stumbled away across the grass.

Garnet ran – not for joy – through the side door and pressed down the safety-lock. Blood pulsed in the side of her mouth. She took the stairs two at a time to her bedroom where she drew the curtains, switched on her PC, and cried.

His teeth on her mouth hadn't hurt *that* much. But it was such a weird thing to do! Well, she had been rude about his great age, but that had been no excuse. Should she tell Raven? What would be the point? Would she not blame her daughter for cannoning into him? For rudeness?

Garnet put herself to bed without dinner. That will teach them, Ebba and Raven, for leaving her alone to manage her latchkey life. '*The world has gone mad,*' she remembered from *The Crucible*. And so it had, since a man occupied the cottage next door.

At two am she woke and crawled to the window, wondering about her mother's whereabouts. The idea that she might have gone next door made Garnet very upset. A fox barked in the scrub and the dog next door responded in kind. A vixen under the trees, crying out for her skulk of foxes? Seasons must matter to foxes, and for all she knew they bit each other when mating.

Garnet's skin crawled at the memory of the neighbour grabbing her. She touched her fingers to her lips. How could her mother bear his hands or mouth on her? But perhaps things were different this time. Perhaps Raven was in control; perhaps she wanted something else from him. Garnet leapt away from the window and rushed downstairs.

While she ransacked her mother's empty room, she found things, evidence — a recipe for Emmenagogue Brew. Penny Royal leaves and blue cohosh, tansy flowers and a quart jar, the writing looped in her mother's graceful cursive. Steaming cupfuls could produce a profuse menstrual flow in sensitive women. Emmenagogue sounded like a Swiss cheese. She looked it up in Ebba's brick of a dictionary.

Emmenagogue also brought on menstrual flow. Who would want that? Garnet had suspicions. When her grandmother's snoring stopped, she fled, carrying the notes to her room. In bed reading with her torch, she found an unspeakable parsley cure for *late* periods. Up to four cups a day of an infusion of tansy flowers and leaves could also be drunk the week before menstruation was due. Ebba grew Tansy. The little yellow buttons lay right beneath the noses of the roses. Companion planting. Blue Cohosh.

March felt interminable. Next day at lunchbreak the sun beat down and burnt her neck. During PE, old Gilly jogged around the cricket pitch while the class ran the outside lane of the oval – then, on command of his whistle, demanded sprints and interval training. At least he had kept them out of class until almost three o'clock — no Geography — YES! The Year Nine boys ran back and forth to the toilets, perving as they passed girls in running shorts and singlets. Cody and Garnet chiacked at the rainwater tank outside the Home-Ec building, guzzled water and poured cups of it over their heads.

Two boys crowded them at the taps. Hip and shouldered them. So not funny. Year Nine boys were feral. Thank God, she'd been accelerated for most classes.

Garnet flicked water. 'Piss off.' Loud. Invited staff intervention.

'Witch water, witch water!' The boys fall to the ground, pretending to fit, faint and die. Through an open classroom door, Year Nine girls hooted with delight.

Surfy boys with excess hormones turned up – FOMO – 'Hot, hot, hot. Claps from the cool people. You will never stop our sense of fun.'

Had they even gone to class after lunch?

'Yes, it's hot, morons,' Garnet responded as scathingly as she could in a wet singlet and no bra. 'Go ride a dolphin.'

Year Twelves free-ranged around the yard. They had special privileges. Zane and Lyndon slouched against the corner of the library, way too chilled to get involved. Zane openly packed his next cone. Thanks for nothing. And Zoe Eddington going for it with one of the surf rats behind the science lab.

'Get a room,' Garnet yelled across the quadrangle at her. Zoe looked up, seemingly unaware that his bristles had scraped her chin red raw. Gross.

'Get on your broom!' Zoe yelled back. What was it with the witch thing?! Bloody Ebba, bloody Raven. Perhaps studying *The Crucible* had made the Year Tens hysterical. Now the drama teacher wanted to stage the play. And Garnet had never suffered such serious harassment.

Cody tugged at her arm. 'Come for a smoke.'

Garnet eyed the shade below the pepper trees. Wondered if a reefer could normalise school relations. Why should she? Schools should provide safe spaces for all students. Zane smirked. Displeased by the fracas, Lyndon hived off. Hated trouble. Thanks for being there for me, guys.

Cody pointed to Gilly fagging outside the school gates, just off school premises. Excellent modelling, Sir.

'Back to class, girls,' he called, clicking his fingers at them.

When Cody walked ahead to class, Garnet's tummy churned. She hauled her bag from her locker and crawled under the now deserted rainwater, tank stand to finish reading Drako's printed study notes on

The Crucible until the bus came. What should she do about her family? Love them / Hate them / Love them / Hate them…

At home, Garnet planned to give the neighbour's car wide berth. She walked along the driveway, stopping only briefly to bark back at the dog. Another mouthful of something disgusting dangled from his fangs. Unpleasant surprises increasingly filled her life. Like the owl pinioned against the grille of Branwell's bull-bar. One of the bird's wings had crumpled behind the other and its yellow eyes stared bleakly past her. Blood trickled from its broken neck. Poor little Boobook. As if someone wouldn't notice an owl swooping out of nowhere and splattering across the front of his car. Bang! How tacky to leave it there — like a trophy — or was he just plain careless?

She found Raven seated on a kitchen stool, reading, and drinking mint tea. 'Garnet, you're looking terribly athletic,' her mother said, glancing up from her book.

'I hate school.'

'I don't believe that.' Her mother sighed, raised her eyebrows at her own cynical joke. 'There are other options if you can hack them.'

Garnet ignored the last thing. 'How come you're home so early?'

'Quiet day. I made seventeen dollars before lunch and read all afternoon. No one came to relieve me of my boredom, so I left.'

'That was it for the day?'

'No money in books.'

'Raven, the man next door killed an owl. It's still espaliered on his car.'

'Sad.' Raven disappeared behind her eyes somewhere.

Garnet wanted to shake her. 'He doesn't care. He invites the big birds to kill his pigeons, you know.'

'Nature can be cruel.'

No one home. She wouldn't tell her mother about yesterday and how a human bit her lip; no, she would not. 'I've seen him late at night. He sets pigeons flying up out of the cage. They flap and flap in a big mob above the roof. He uses a leather glove that goes right up his arm to throw one of the birds of prey up high in the air and go after them.'

Blooding a caged bird? Had she really seen that?

Raven stared through her. 'Like a sacrifice, you think?' Her mother was so literal.

'Sometimes a peregrine sits on top of the yew tree. They know when to come. At the perfect moment, it dive-bombs. *Caccccarccccarccccarack*.' Garnet threw her arms about and stood over her mother. 'The pigeon squawks and the peregrine tears it to pieces.'

Raven remained motionless. Excesses of nature did not shock her. 'I warned you to take care.'

Garnet wanted to scream at her about taking care of herself. What had she been up to the night before? A mother should be smarter than a moth flying towards any light. She mooched upstairs feeling hopeless. The three-bad-luck-things-in-a-row had happened.

After her diary entry she checked her email — kimmer@paisley. com.uk. Well, it could just sit there for a bit. Right click — she put a block on Zane for starters. Pity she couldn't do it in real life. Soon her screen had more windows open than a set of louvres.

Ting
> Garnet: Cody. Have you ever had mail from Paisley?
> Garnet: Daisy, ever heard of kimmer from Paisley?
> Garnet: Kendra, kimmer, you got them on your mail list?'
> Garnet: Mick, Paisley, heard of it?
> No, no, no.

Ting
> Paisley, notification:
> You have successfully received c:/bairns-gey wet things/witch from Paisley. You may want to scan this with an anti-virus program before you play this .mov

Film 3 presented in sepia colours, like the photos of Papa James Miller. In the first two seconds the shawl girl uprooted plants of some kind and dropped them in a basket. She stopped to smell her fingertips, but you couldn't see her face. Then in a half-second flash, she hovered over another girl writhing with her knees up on a rough bed. The girl screamed — face contorted — a surety the scene depicted must be childbirth. Garnet recognised it from movies and the gruesome health ed videos shown at school. But then again it could be period pain.

She hit the rewind button — no response — scene froze. Control/alt/delete — gone — and no trace on the task bar or in the trash. Just as weird as ever. She flicked back to her list. Zane and Cody had dropped out.

Garnet: Lyndon, how can a film clip self-destruct? Like disappear once you've watched them.

Lyndon: Wot?

Garnet: I've received 3 .mov files. I play them once & they're gone.

Lyndon: Check the trash?

Garnet: No go. Not there.

Lyndon: Ask who sent them to you.

Garnet: Can't. Anon. kimmer@paisley.com.uk I have no idea who that is.

Lyndon: you wrote and asked them directly?

Garnet: No response.

Lyndon: Sicko?

Garnet: Can't tell. I don't know anyone in Paisley. Well one old aunt and I've never met her. It's in Scotland.

Lyndon: Are you okay?

Garnet: Sure I am.

Garnet stuffed some tissues in an empty Pringles canister and went downstairs for dinner. Fennel soup — divine — and garlic bread from the bread maker. She hadn't seen the moon for days. Light sprayed from the hills to the north. Things were moving around outside. Grumpiness turned to curiosity. She unblocked Zane and read the last message.

Chapter Six

FIRE: PASSION

Garnet flicked on her bedside lamp, heaved the phone out from under her bed, and read the message.

I'm outside. I know where you live. Come outside.
Zaney boy.

Gaia, it was two am. She peered out the window and could just make out his car idling fifty metres down the road. He hadn't been lying. Pulling on track pants and t-shirt and carrying her shoes, she padded past the magnolias and through the front gate. Zane cut the engine and bounded across the road grinning. Such a control freak.

'You bingled your car.'

'Everyone gets upset sometimes. And you thought I was perfect.' He put an arm around her shoulders. 'Take me to the poison garden.'

'What are you talking about?' Garnet was damn sure she hadn't mentioned their garden to him. As if she would. Out of recent personal interest, she had been keeping careful notes in a folder titled Herbs and Poisons on the desktop of her computer. Puzzling over the depth and

57

breadth of Raven and Ebba's pottiness was one thing: Zane knowing about it another.

Of course *he* would be interested, bent soul that he was, likely he'd dreamed about poisoning his father. But then she doubted him that bad – absent dad – just trying to get attention. But how did he know about the plants? The Zonta ladies blabbing? Good thing they didn't have a cat. Then they'd be completely fitted out for witchcraft. But Ebba would never tolerate the wanton killing of birds; which made the new neighbour a contradiction.

Zane pulled a bottle from the inside pocket of his coat, swigged from it, and placed it against her lips. She briefly hesitated. Raven gulped at life, why shouldn't Garnet drink too? But why was *he* here this time? An argument with his parents? The drink tasted sweet, warming, strong. Some kind of liqueur. It dribbled down her chin and he kissed softly where it spilled. A frisson of excitement lit her mood. She turned her head and eyeballed the neighbour's dog, barking on his chain. Zane pulled at her hand, making her heart thump.

'Take me, show me.'

'What?'

'The garden. Show me the plants.'

'What do you know about Raven's garden? Rubbish passed on by Cody?'

'No. You must have told me. Drink a drop more.' He pressed the flask against her lips.

Garnet had jumped warm from her bed into the friendly dark. Alcohol slid through her veins. Always unpredictable, Zane cast his eyes left and right, taking in the wavering lines of opium poppies, young foxgloves, narcissus and arum lilies, as he drew her towards the river. Why did he care about plants?

'Why don't you ask for dates properly?'

'Too conventional for a witch like you.'

'Don't give me that witch bullshit, Zane. You know I'm getting witch crap at school and I hate it.'

'But why? That's the question.' He limped towards the pomegranate tree and picked a ripe one.

She sighed. 'It's Raven and Ebba. They don't go to Nutra-Medic parties, buy the *Women's Weekly*, work in the footy canteen, play the pokies, talk in the main street, blah, blah, blah... They're aliens. It's just like Drako said in English. They're always going to be picked on, just because no men have legal access to their bodies. In the old days they'd get blamed for everything — crops failing, cows losing their milk, the common cold.'

'Why are you so fired up?'

'You're not walking properly. What's wrong with your leg?'

'I fell. Let's stick to you, poppet.'

'Poppet.' Garnet paused, considered the word, left it right where he'd left it, and continued. 'I've been reading about witch trials online. They sound barbaric.'

'True, true.' Zane covered her hand with his, moved the bottle back to his mouth and quaffed a large mouthful. 'About body access...' His hand snaked around her waist. 'I found an excellent letter saved on my father's computer, to *your* mother. He sounded quite annoyed with her.'

'Is that why you fell?' She prodded his knee, making him wince. 'Did he find out about you snooping?

'No.'

'In any case, someone should report him for harassing patients.' Garnet swigged angrily from the bottle again. 'Maybe me.'

'Hey!' Zane gathered her in, nudging her mouth with his, and then opened his lips against hers. His breath tasted smoky, sweet with alcohol. His mouth moved over her neck and face. She licked her lips. Raven might be right about some things. Hands slid and tongues compelled, and Garnet obeyed some instinctive choreography of the body.

Night smells filled the garden – flowers, animals on the move. A mephitic fog rolled along the river. A feral cat skirled. Desire. She liked the word desire. It rolled off your tongue and into your mind. *No, no, no, no, no.*

It felt even more potent commingled with fear and a chill breeze that rose off the river. Did Zane want to screw her in her mother's garden – compete with his father – hold it over Garnet at school? Did he know she was young for her year level, but assume that she knew things because of her mother? He ducked his head to touch the base of her throat with the tip of his tongue, making her tremble. Moved his head down her body, nudging and mouthing, pushing her top above the band of her track pants.

'What are you doing?' she said.

'Searching for marks – birthmarks, freckles, scars – signs on your skin.'

She smacked at his hand. 'I'm not afraid of your bullshit.'

He looked up at her as if asking a question before he pressed against her again. Against her better judgment, wanting to lie down with him – was that natural? The moon cowered behind roiling cloud. And now, she'd lost all conviction. He had rattled her. Completely untrustworthy.

And how had he known about Raven's plants? He was clever, too clever, but had he lost interest in the garden or was he just giving her a line? Angry with his father, or competing with him?

The nicotiana, the datura, the evening primrose, the night phlox; the white night things shone as if they watched her. Garnet felt spooked. 'I'm going in.'

She pulled away from him, brushed down her trackies and moved towards the gate as if to see him off the premises.

'Garnet, stay.'

'No. Toss this.' She picked up the horseshoe on the gate and passed it to him. Zane threw it. It clanked against the post. An upstairs light flicked on.

'Bad luck, you lose – tosser,' she said, and couldn't explain her sudden anger, even to herself. Wind chimes brushed against her face and tinkled.

From a sea-grass chair on the veranda, she watched his retreat. She leant over the balustrade, saw Lyndon smoking on the roadside, and felt annoyed with herself. Had he seen anything? What must he think of her – that she behaved just like any of Zane's obedient, willing girls? What would Zane tell him they had done? She slid between the shadows on the verandah and tiptoed upstairs.

Unreal, a fourth kimmer message at three am. If she could just get one on her hard drive and play around with it! The clip ran short and loud. If Ebba woke there would even more trouble.

Heart drumming, she fumbled for the volume, then watched a girl shaking her fist, pounding it against the back of another girl, who, face obscured by a dark shawl, herded cows with a long stick. The sound of lowing filled Garnet's bedroom as the girls rushed across the screen between the cows. Had she entered a witch platform game? Were the girls quarrelling? She wondered if a narrative would emerge.

In Film 1, a hysterical girl runs from the bush into a graveyard; dogs bark, she cries, falls in heap in front of wooden cross. Why?

In Film 2 Same girl, scared witless, backs up against a wall, under attack perhaps; she looks injured

In Film 3 she gathers herbs, then tends a woman in labour.

And in Film 4, she hits someone and herds cows.

The shawls, the scarves, the long dresses, all looked otherworldly. Did the sender keep Garnet's hours? Of course, the difference between Australia and Paisley was about twelve hours. Perhaps it was daylight now in Paisley.

To take her mind off everything, she played a bit of *Half-Life 2* – would they ever develop *Half-Life 3*? – in which a girl could kill. Not that it meant much when you only saw your hands and a gun. But Garnet liked running past people and using the arrow keys to avoid getting shot.

Next door, a car door slammed, and Garnet peered between her curtains at two young men loading boxes into a station wagon. What was Branwell Renshaw up to in the middle of the night? She crawled under her bedcovers and experimentally sucked her thumb. Tried to concentrate on more pleasurable aspects of the evening.

Zane disturbed her. That was a fact. But... she punched her pillow and rolled on her back, replaying in her mind, the parts when his hands and his mouth had touched her body. A galaxy of Fluro stickers danced across her ceiling. She felt confused. Hysterical with tiredness. Damn

Zane. What did he – what did she – want? Tomorrow she would try to work both out.

Garnet was not a morning person and slumped over her toast at breakfast until Ebba nagged at her to straighten up.

'I have been visualising your source of pain,' she said.

Garnet wondered if Ebba just fished. Did she mean Zane or the neighbour? She decided to play dumb. 'Good-oh. Can you pass the butter, Eb? I'm so stuffed.'

'Sleep is what you need, my girl, and justice. Don't worry, I will make a spell that binds.'

'Thanks. Is there anything I can do to help *you*?'

Ebba reached over to light a poplar-leaf, beeswax candle. 'I have cut myself off safely, but don't cross the running stream today.'

'You mean the river?'

The match flared. 'I cannot say. Everything comes back threefold. My intent is good, but you should always take care, darling.'

'Ebba, could you possibly give me a lift into town? Unfortunately, I have missed the yellow motorised thing.' Anyone could speak in riddles.

Ebba nodded, gathering plates and cups. 'My first appointment is at eleven.' How could people be afraid of Ebba when she was so well-meaning? Not a nasty bone in her body.

Garnet sighted Zane at the end of lunchtime, in the reference section in the Resource Centre, slouched over a dog-eared copy of *Hyper*.

She glared at him. 'I want to talk to you.'

'Not a problem. After school at the Shell.'

Who else would message someone at two am and expect them to jump – well, wriggle actually – and then be too superior to talk to them at school? And *then* offer to meet at a servo!

'You are something else.'

'Settle!'

'Selfish.'

'No, don't like shellfish.'

She stayed back after school to work on her art project until she was sure Zane would have grown tired waiting at the Shell and left. Then she fronted up to his house. When he answered the door, she pushed inside — rudeness plus. Ebba would purse her lips if she knew.

Thanks to his mother's penchant for expensive décor magazines and his father's income, Zane lived in faux New York. Garnet took in the minimalist silver and cream design lines and fingered the good blonde wood. More than likely his mother made her little pet's bed and shampooed his hair.

'Where's your cell?' She felt desperate to check out his PC and destabilise his confidence. Now he would think *she* was after *him*, and it served him right.

'Follow, smexy girl.'

More likely dead-set keen to hide her away in case his folks heard them. Glancing behind him, Zane surveyed the passage, then quietly closed his door. His room stank of grungy dirty-socks and junk-food. But then, so did hers. Porno magazines lay open on his bed. Different.

The sounds of little kids roaring around the neighbour's back yard grounded her. Sliding onto his chair, she whizzed his mouse back and forth, to view recent files. Face cast down, he allowed this but slipped in behind her, arms firm around her waist head nuzzling her neck. She swung her head and used both hands to loosen his arms.

Zane winced and tugged at his sleeves to cover a heavy bruise.

'Have you had another accident?'

'Shame job. If I'm not consistently in the ninety-fifth percentile, my arsehole father commandeers the car.'

'Shh! That's a lot of pressure.' She stroked his face with her fingertips, before she turned back to his folders. Thank Gaia for speed-reading.

'Love a coffee,' she murmured, moving the cursor rapidly over his music files, school subject folders and digital photos. 'History projects?' This one looked full of big fat files. He moved his hand over hers on the mouse and experimentally walked his other hand across her thigh.

'Let me look?' she begged, pushing off his hand. Bad move.

'Leave it. Just something Lyndon and I are mucking around with.'

He folded her hand in his and lifted it against his cheek. Kissed her. He tasted like corn chips. 'Come on, and I'll make you a coffee.'

'Five more minutes. Please.'

He looked glum again and hung his head. She swivelled the chair back to face the desk. 'Cool screen saver, if you like checking all your facial pores for acne every time you log in. Switch on your camera. It must take high-res shots.'

'I don't think so. My mother bought it overseas and I don't like other people touching it.'

'Speaking of mothers. What about mine? What's this dirt you have on her? Extra kidney?'

'Actually, nothing much. Trying to get your attention, and Cody told me something her mother told her. A nurse sighted my father not forty kilometres from here, sharing fruit of the vine in a boutique winery with your mother. Deep meaningful looks exchanged.'

'Flesh-pressing?'

'Hinted at. So that's a precedent, don't you think?' He fiddled with her zip.

Garnet disentangled herself and scooped up her backpack.

'Dunno. I've changed my mind about coffee. About everything. I've organised to meet Cody at the bookshop at five. Not only do we need to talk about her relationship with you but we're working on the physics assignment together.'

Zane trailed after her to the front door, hung on the doorstep, arms laced through the wrought iron balustrade, hair licking his eyes. 'Trust.'

'You've got to be kidding.'

He looked pale and skinny. Had she ever thought about whether he was happy? Guess not. Well, not often. If his father belted him – and she still didn't know the details – the room must be his bolthole, where he plotted futile revenge. Garnet hitched her bag higher up onto her shoulders and walked out onto the footpath. Flipped her fingers over her shoulder.

'Letter for you,' said Raven, passing an envelope over the messy counter of the bookshop. 'Scotland.' Cody had disappeared into the popular Romance section of the shop. Garnet ripped the envelope open.

My Dear Garnet,

Your grandmother tells me that you are interested in our family history and in Paisley. I am so pleased. You may like to see some of my old snaps. Although I believe that most young people now use the Internet, if I can be of any assistance to you, by gathering books or pamphlets from the library, please let me know.

I am afraid I do not know much about computers, and I am far too old to learn. The best thing would be to persuade your grandmother to bring you on a trip to meet me. For many years she has promised to come home to visit us but, of course, your mother has been quite unwell.

Today is Saturday and it will be very quiet for me. Early this morning, I walked along the shore. The tide was a long way out and I gathered pretty stones. Lately, I have been watching a family of swans diving for food. As it is spring, many cygnets have hatched. Remember from the Hans Christian Anderson's story that they have brown feathers and make very ugly ducklings. Please tell Ebba that I so enjoyed receiving the beautiful Australian bird calendar at Christmas time...

Garnet felt her mood lift. All data. Potentially useful. She felt sure that unless she was a very accomplished liar, this old lady could not be a computer hacker. She shoved the letter in her blazer pocket, resolving to nag Ebba about a Scottish holiday as soon as possible.

Raven closed the shop, and without further words or social niceties drove Cody and Garnet home. Ebba worked in her room. The neighbour seemed to be in absentia, and Raven wove peacefully to the sound of Elgar.

The moon rose late, a pale coagulated yolk, behind the trees. As it moved, its markings changed to look like kelp draped across its surface. The moon could be whatever you wanted, but always feminine. Everywhere else, the sky looked clean and full of bright spaces. The saucepan and her constellatory mates the emu and the lion shone brightly. Garnet began a moon diary while Cody pounded the keyboard, finishing up the physics. Then she fronted her.

'What's this crap about Raven and Zane's father?'

Cody had the grace to look uncomfortable. 'Sorry, babe. Forget it. Zane's dad has a bad rep anyway. Should hear what the nurses at the hospital say. A few of them dumped their husbands for him, and he screwed them round. Then they lost their jobs. This is gospel according to my very Christian mother.'

'I didn't know doctors were allowed to do that. So, Raven too?'

'Briefly. She gave *him* the flick and it didn't go down well. More details available from Mother's Wednesday tennis group.'

Garnet sighed and twisted her hair on top of her head; then let the pile collapse all over her face.

'Stop talking to him about my family or we're done.'

'Okay. Seemed harmless, but I hear you.'

'You know that's not true.'

'Forgive me.' Cody squeezed her hand. 'Are you coming out soon, dear Yeti?'

Garnet blew air up into her fringe to clear her face and climbed across to tickle Cody's back through her tracksuit top. 'Five minutes, then swap. Zane's acting weird with me. It would piss me off if it had anything to do with Raven and his dad.'

'Use him, chuck him. Like your mum did his dad?'

'Even if she did, stupid game. Why would anyone bother?'

'Boredom. Raven must hate living here. She's so beautiful.'

Garnet bit her lip. Hrm. Maybe. 'But now, I really want to know about kimmer@paisley.net.uk.'

'Another email?'

'Four clips, total. If another one arrives, I won't try to open it. I'll just reply if it will let me. *Stop spamming me. Get a life.* That's what I'll write.'

'Could be someone at school?'

'I think they pay their provider bill in Paisley. Might be here on holiday? I need to check it out.'

'Mmm.'

'The awful thing is that whoever it is, they must know things about me, and about Raven and Ebba. Or why else would they pick on me about witches? Family? Got it? Please, please don't flap your mouth with Zane or anyone. About us — me? About the things we talk about?'

'Only when they drug me.' Cody giggled. 'Kidding.'

Garnet stared her down. 'Nothing about me or my family. We're friends. Boys think they're entitled to do and know anything they please.'

'Got the memo.' Cody reached out to hug her. 'I'll tickle you and then let's get back to your internet problem.'

'It's a UK domain name.'

'Trickier then.'

'But, on the dark, dark net, anyone can hide their country of origin.'

'Roll over. It's your turn. What's "kimmer", their name?' Cody ran her fingers along Garnet's shoulders and down the middle of her back.

'It's an old word for witch. I looked it up on the net.'

'Message.' Cody leapt up and tossed Garnet her phone. 'It's one am. Who is it?'

'Bloody Zane. He's outside again. Wants to know if we'll go for a burn in his car.'

'Let's, eh? My life is so terminally boring.'

'Terminal is what it could be riding with him. Have you seen his clapped-out pride and joy?'

'Pleeze. Are we still talking about his car?'

Garnet slapped at her. 'Alright, but only if you take the front seat and keep your hands off the go button.'

'Fair. We'll have fun. You and me.' She pushed a lock of hair away from Garnet's eyes and leapt up, face lit.

They bailed out of the bedroom, legs over the sill and down the drainpipe, because Cody said she had always wanted to escape an upstairs bedroom that way. When Garnet's shoe fell into the garden, she hoped to Gaia that Ebba and Raven stayed asleep, at least until they got away. The moon cast bright light over the yard. If Cody giggled again, she would kick her bum. Order had been restored.

Goody Nurse in *The Crucible* was right that children go through their *silly seasons. A child's spirit is like a child, you can never catch it by running after it; you must stand still, and, for love, it will soon itself come back.* Garnet would love Cody forever.

They found Zane and Lyndon leaning up against the car on the edge of the valley road, beers in hand, talking quietly.

'We're not doing that "boys in the front girls, in the back thing",' Garnet blurted out. 'Code, get in there with Zane.' *Her choice*, she bet he was thinking.

'Do you always have to be in control?' he asked.

'It's my preference. You?' Garnet slid into the back seat next to Lyndon and reached over for a swig of his beer.

Zane accelerated rapidly. He thought he was so damned decadent. His father probably had the same Doris Day-movie recipe — hot cars, loud music, smooth liquor and willing chicks.

Lyndon slung an arm around her. He must be a teens-bit whizzed.

'I've been reading this guy Derrida, about deconstruction. Do you believe that a text is anything that conveys meaning? That any communication can be considered a text?' he slurred.

'I think if you keep drinking, you'll self-destruct. But I'll run with the text thing. Tell me more, boy genius.'

'He wanted...'

'Who?' She grabbed at his beer.

'Jacques Derrida.' He slapped her fingers down. 'He wanted to be a professional soccer player, but he wasn't good enough. He wrote forty books instead.'

'What a loss to the world.'

They ducked their heads together in a spasm of laughter.

Garnet fell in with the rhythm of the car as Zane whipped around the bends, screeching his tyres, turning the car this way and then the other, all the way to the next town. Yankalilla was as dead as a doornail, three lights on, one cat, no traffic on the road, and one lonely jay walker. If only Cody wouldn't squeal so much. It made Zane even more idiotic. Garnet could see them passing a joint back and forth in the front, her friend's face open and too agreeable, smoke settling round her face like an aura. Time to keep watch.

She lolled against Lyndon's chest, still trying to connect with the idea that all information could be meaningless, and everyone had to construct their own reality. Lyndon was kind, a good friend, low-risk — so far. Zane was like something you dropped in a drink — could go any which way. Hyped Cody dampened Garnet's mood.

Thoughts of high-impact interactions with pale moonlit gums, of rolling out of control, and of the car searing along the bitumen and sliding into the river jangled her mood. She felt tired, and in danger of losing her nerve. Who cared that they were out on a lonely night, just missing possums and foxes skittering away from the light?

Shit-scared feelings enveloped her. As they approached her turnoff she leaned forward and tapped Zane on the shoulder. 'We're out of here. Thanks for your scintillating company.'

The reality, textual or not, was that when Garnet and Cody bumped about in the dark hall, whispering, giggling, high maybe on being high, Raven appeared, performing a reasonable impersonation of a mother.

Garnet burped. Beer did that to her. 'Don't say a word. Don't do it. Don't go there, Mother.' She giggled.

'Take Cody upstairs, Garnet, and place a bowl beside her bed. I'll speak to you in the morning.'

'Funny, Raven. That is sooo funny.'

Cody slept on her back, breathing adenoidally. Garnet woke at three am and crept to her computer. It hummed and pinged. Animated cats marched on their hind legs across her desktop. Macabre. After two laps, the fourth cat in line, padded to just above the start button, hissed and rolled its bulbous eyes at her. A hallucination, a new virus, or had someone hacked into Garnet's computer to stalk her? Perhaps they'd ridden in on the last film clip and latched on to her hard drive.

Chapter Seven

MABON: REVERSING CURSES

By Saturday, Garnet had reorganised all her files, dragged them into new folders, renamed them, and protected them with passwords offline. If someone had hacked into her system, they were doing it online.

Well, obviously. No one could access her bedroom, could they...? Until she changed all her passwords, they might have found out a lot about her. Someone could have read her diary — mega cringe.

They would have to be bloody clever to get in now. She would tell no one about her changed security, not even her best friend. Especially not. But then, even if she could hack computers, why would Cody bother? Garnet told her everything.

Lyndon could probably hack in, but he was so nice. He wouldn't. Surely. And Daisy and Kendra — why would they bother? Mick — he had a life. Would a clever third-world hacker find her interesting? Short answer: no.

Had one person sent the film clips *and* hacked in? Personal information could be traded. List brokers sold names and addresses. People made a fortune trading data that was none of their business.

Garnet cut and pasted text and pictures, on Paisley and the history of witches, into various folders. It seemed appropriate to plan more research on their garden during autumn equinox. 'Poison garden' had only ever been a throw-away line to shock Cody, and presumably it had worked, because she must have told Zane.

Garnet had always assumed that Ebba did whatever she liked in an ever-constricting world. Raven acted differently, her cortex like a cluster bomb, its brain waves firing off at random moments. If someone tut-tutted about this plant or that, Raven would rush to slide her trowel under the tiny, tenuous, self-seeded green shoot and take a cutting, slip it away.

Was everything a matter of intent? Many dangerous things were beautiful, but not all beautiful things could be taken in lethal doses. Why had Zane pretended so much interest, when his father must have a grab bag of capsules, pills and substances to hand? He could experiment any time he liked. Was it that instinctively he looked for an edge, or got off on unsettling everyone? Did he have a particular problem with her? Was that what the kissing was about?

Ebba had been cleaning the yard all day. Garnet watched her cutting back untidy elder branches. Elderberries and flowers were edible and could help with circulation, sinusitis, colds and catarrh. As well as elderberry wine or champagne, they could be made into an excellent caterpillar spray.

The rest of the tree was poisonous. When eaten, seeds created cyanide inside the body. Agatha Christie, who frequently found her murder weapons in gardens, had used cyanide in ten novels and four stories. Garnet had devoured all the books at twelve, but had only recently begun to think about them again. For at least an hour, she followed Ebba around, made lists, asked questions, wrote notes, and cross-checked everything.

Mugwort – wormwood to Harry Potter devotees – became most potent just before it flowered. Ebba mixed mugwort with sage, sandalwood and rosemary, to relax and release her subconscious. The mixture opened psychic channels and created visions. *Soo* very Ebba. Apparently, it should be cut at a waning moon for scrying. Scrying meant seeing things in the future, visions unbidden and best facilitated by a bowl of water. But Ebba had never had the knack.

Sometimes, Garnet worried that she, her granddaughter, did. Lately, everything had seemed to resonate with meaning and consequence, most puzzlingly the little boy who appeared behind her in the mirror like an aureole. Mixed with penny-royal and southwood, mugwort could be infused in wine, bathed in or drunk as tea at bedtime to bring sweet dreams. Had drinking Ebba's tea unsettled her and brought on the image of the boy? Living way out of town, she had always wanted a brother or sister.

Mugwort could be used to bring on menstruation. Garnet flumped onto the lawn and closed her eyes. As if anyone would want to bring on menstruation. Cursed once a month was enough for her. A breeze tickled her face as she thought about her fear of becoming more like her mother, who never seemed happy for long.

Ebba and Raven were not on Garnet's wavelength. And increasingly, their plantings puzzled her. Surely her mother didn't have a life-long need to bring her period on. Garnet doubted that Ebba even had periods anymore. When Garnet had bled the first time at the age of thirteen, they had given her a garnet ring, made celebratory noises, and held up a goblet of raspberry cordial. It had seemed like a con at the time, periods being both painful and inconvenient, but she had nevertheless been chuffed that she had entered some hallowed women's inner circle. Raspberries fresh cut from canes and blood were entirely different.

When two ailing chooks lost their heads to Ebba's axe, Garnet stood on the woodheap and wailed. Watching the poor headless things run demented around the yard put her at odds with her grandmother. Even though she didn't want sickly birds to die a painful death, the bloody-feathered, dirtied scraps of life pulsing and spurting at Ebba's feet nearly did her in. Blood disturbed her. Killing animals made her squeamish. She didn't, however, believe plants held feelings and liked to help Ebba drag and rake fallen branches, prunings, leaves and rubbish into a bonfire pile beside the poplars.

Over the years, all three of them knelt reverently to drop tubes of blue gums, spotted gums and river red gums into the soft mud of the woodlot across the river. Living / Dying / Life/ Death / Ebba / Raven.

As she lay on the grass, a breeze started up and the datura flowers began to sway. Secretly afraid of them, Garnet also liked their mystery. Perhaps what she really liked was overthinking about darkness and danger. When hacked to the ground, poisoned or, according to Raven, chain-sawed, datura refused to die. Despite the heat, they continued flowering. On blistering hot days, the plants frizzled in the soil, the pale bells singed brown like hot-ironed silk and then dried back to a fragile crepe before they dropped. The leaves defiantly curled and closed to stay alive. The trunk cauterised itself until only small round nubs of green remained. Each plant held itself strong till water came, or moisture in the next cool breeze. Were datura really fertilised by bats?

Once, Garnet had carried a flower inside to the chopping board and used a vegetable knife to slit open its soft stomach. The green parts were immature. It had been hard to imagine the soft white length of the bell-shaped flute, now delicately enfolded, its stamen like pale babies in utero.

Garnet went inside. On her way to her keyboard, she snaffled some lemon verbena and chamomile biscuits to munch while she read at her computer. Imbibed, datura leaves brought psychoactive effects. At night the plant dispensed an intoxicating fragrance. In 1676, a group of Jamestown soldiers went insane after cooking and ingesting it. A vasodilator, whatever that was, datura enlarged veins and heightened blood flow.

Garnet had once rubbed plant matter between two fingers and raised it to her nose like a lady taking snuff but had experienced no dizziness. Stories about colonial Indian women who seethed with passion for light-skinned men interested her. They gave datura to their husbands, who became wide-eyed and stupefied, while the previously powerless wives made love to pale men in front of them. Bored, perhaps. Garnet decided she would not inhale. Would not do *stupefied*. Was she kidding herself?

When Raven had planted the first tree Ebba warned her that they were dangerous for babies. That her daughter might chew on a leaf, suck at flowers, or play with seeds. Garnet felt sure that had she shown any interest, Ebba would have grubbed the tree out herself, but more generally she took the view that the world was full of poisons, if people were mad or sad enough to seek them out.

Chapter Eight

AUTUMNAL EQUINOX, 21 MARCH

Raven must have stayed at the bookshop until after six. By dusk, Garnet and Ebba had built up their pile of garden rubbish and set it alight. Ebba cast the circle, entered from the northeast, and kissed Garnet first on each cheek and then on her mouth. When the first flames licked the air, the neighbour's dog howled, and a nest of baby rabbits erupted from beneath the crackling pile.

'Hot cross buns,' cried Ebba, casting round the edges with her stick. Evil woman.

'Very funny. Not.' Garnet squeezed her arm.

'We'll keep our secrets in. What a bonny blaze.'

Neighbours' fires plumed along the road. Soon it would be too wet to burn. Valley householders had viewed the loury sky and seized the last chance to get rid of their rubbish.

'I thought I heard Raven.' Garnet turned her head hopefully. Would she be in a mood to be included?

Ebba passed her honey cake and ale and began tying knots in a length of ribbon, binding and releasing energy, reciting verse.

'Good will come, Garnet, from the dark light, from ruin, only blessings.'

'I bet you'd like to dance, Ebba.'

'It would be fun to whip up a bit of energy, but.'

'Let's do the paper thing.'

'Surely, get some pens and paper.'

Garnet scrambled to her feet and climbed the slope to the house. Dark wispy clouds moved across the sky, signalling change. Half-visible, the moon spilled silver. Rusty whirls of smoke swirled across its face. Raven had angled her car in the driveway, at cross purposes to his, as if she'd jumped out of it in a hurry and gone straight over. Garnet's heart sank as she tiptoed, trying not to crunch the gravel, towards the narrow line of light at his window and peered in.

Together. Facing each other across a wooden refectory table. Oil glistened on his chin as he ate a small bird using his fingers – perhaps a pigeon – tossed back red wine and angled his aristocratic head to smile at her mother. Raven looked serious – sober even – beautiful, her fringed scarf draped across her shoulders, red ankle boots demurely crossed below her chair, hair skewered on top of her head with a knitting needle. Ignoring her food, she was doing all the talking. Holding up a book cover: *Moral Hazard* by Kate someone? Excellent book title. And why hadn't Raven smelled the bonfire and come out to join her family?

Garnet mooched into her house, then back out to the bonfire with paper, pens, and three of Raven's scarves to dress the elder tree.

'Is Raven home yet?' asked Ebba.

'Been, gone, mark her place. So, write.' Garnet passed the paper. Sometimes she and Ebba liked to muck around, talk nonsense, like familial animals grunted to acknowledge each other's presence. They scribbled, crossed out, rewrote, and tossed their paper desires into the fire, where they caught and fluttered up.

'What is your weakness then, Ebba?'

'I would like to avail myself of tears.'

'Do you need to wish for that?'

'It seems I do. Daft bitch I am.' Ebba laughed. 'And you?'

'I want to lose weight.'

Ebba looked concerned.

'Jeez. I'm joking. Overwrite. Take me off the mailing list for anorexia and bulimia support. You know, I just need to get a grip. I get so smashed out on all the crap in my life that I want to do something destructive, dumb, reactive or destructive. Impulse control must be my next goal.'

'I think you're great. You deal with a lot of difficult things so well. I can see your growth.' Ebba patted her knee. 'Cody could toss that paper wish into our bonfire.'

'Her mother would die if she knew the half of it, and pack her off to a church boarding school.'

'She worries me. But she's a smart young woman, and she has you.'

'Nearly all the girls I know think they'll end up different to their parents. But watch this space... Ebba, does talking about it hurt the magic?'

'Depends on your beliefs. At my age it's hard not to act like a hag and hold on to every bitter thought.'

'Do you think this stuff helps – little ceremonies?'

'Rituals help me focus, find a pathway, concentrate my energies. Peace is more important to me now than opening everything up. I hear too many sad stories at work.'

'Ah yes. Assault, harassment, rape, trauma, followed by depression, dieting, disorder. All ahead of me. Do ceremonies help Raven?'

'Your mother takes what she wants, but I think she's getting better at knowing what she needs. Like the happiness that blesses you.'

'Do you really think I'm happy?'

'Don't you?'

'Thinking hurts. Roll on some new experiences.'

'Of course. We all like *some* new experiences.'

'Night times, I practise dark me.' Garnet screws up her face and weaves her fingers in the air. 'Mad girl in the attic.'

Ebba laughs 'Aim for balance. Kick up a bit, then channel your energy.'

Garnet stretched her legs out on the grass. Leaned back on her hands, head angled, to take in the swiftly-moving sky. The fire – bright orange, red and brown – blazed warm on her shoulders. Something had built in the atmosphere. It felt palpable – as if she might reach out and touch it.

Would Raven come and join them? If only she came alone and not with him.

When thunder tore open the sky and sheets of lightning lit the Mt Alma scarp, Garnet sprang up. The neighbour's horse galloped along the fence-line, head thrown back, whinnying. Cows moved under the trees to shelter from the quickening wind. Rain splashed their faces. Ebba stood up, stretched her arthritic limbs and shook out her crumpled clothing. Little flames whippled across the surface of the low fire. Despite light rain, Ebba hosed it, making sure.

'Bluidy heck. I reek of smoke. And you.'

Queer raspy mews split the air, as the neighbour's birds shifted uneasily on the perches, eyes darting, wings raised. Was her mother planning to stay inside with him all night? After dinner, would they torture themselves on the rowing machines, muscle builders and whirring bikes, or use stupid belts and harnesses? That surely wouldn't suit Raven. They had nothing in common. Couldn't they both see that? Her mother never settled long on any perch. Garnet stared at his chimney spewing smoke and ran across the yard on tiptoe to his front door.

Muddy footprints marked the step; someone else had come to call. Garnet smoothed spare paper onto the shoe track to create a print. Hard copy – dangerous. She would scan it and put it in a folder labelled 'Progress'. 'Clues, Detective Southwood.' She ran across the path to their own cottage. Close behind her, Ebba hung her coat on a hook at the door and turned to kiss Garnet.

'That was fun,' said Garnet, 'especially when I jumped the bonfire to protect our secrets.' Yawning on the stair, she feigned an early night. No point in worrying people. Most adolescents were nocturnal. Plenty of scientific evidence said so.

She opened her playlist but turned the volume low so that Ebba would assume her to be winding down – off to nightie-night – and fall asleep herself. Back and forth to the music, she rocked her chair, applied black lipstick and felt dark, dark, dark. Yes, her mother needed to get a life, but not with someone seriously weird: a bird warden, carnivore, gym junkie. Someone who bit little girls.

The slow-combustion fire hissed in the kitchen. Ebba would have shut it down to simmer till the morning. Rain thrummed; tree branches scrunched harder than broom bristles on the roof.

Rats skittered. Back inside *they* crept, when the weather cooled and summer feed became scarce: armies of marauders, they gnawed through cardboard packets, soft plastic, even electrical wire; shat in cupboards. Garnet shuddered at the scuttle and grind behind skirting boards and above her in ceiling gyprock.

In chat rooms no one knew she was at all disturbed, worried about her mother, or knew that she even had one. Disappearing into a community where lines were blurred and no one cared about age, body shape, gender or race pleased her. It allowed her to construct her own reality. Feeling aggro, she dived into a furious argument with a fantasy nerd about *The Blair Witch Project*. She didn't love the first film but because it was a sleeper lots of overseas dudes were addicted to the nth.

She hit shuffle on her playlist, simultaneously played a few hands of solitaire and searched online for more of Raven's plants. Yew trees were commonly found in churchyards, probably because Christians took over Druid holy places, in the same way that Raven had planted her Yew near a Ngarrindjeri canoe tree site. Best sites were best sites – for river crossings, spirits, and fresh water. Yews grew huge. Ebba's was not full-grown, shaggy with straggly needles and browned-off bits. Bit like her. Bet a dollar that she knew every part of the tree was poisonous and planted it to be obtuse.

Ting

Cody: Are you awake? I'm getting drilled at online chess.

Garnet: Been there, done...

Cody: Yeah. Do you think we'll ever get out of this shithole of a town?

Garnet: I'm grumpy too but no excuse. Are you okay?

Cody: Not really. I think I'm going to choke on Gord. And Lyn. They are the worst parents. We've been blueing all night.

Garnet: It's normal. Chill.

Cody: Can't. Going to implode.

Garnet: Go to bed or you'll blow things. They'll tighten up so much you won't be able to move.

Cody: I know. I know. Love you.

Garnet: Love you.

If their world continued to disappoint them, Garnet and Cody would have to live online with other lost, bored souls – within months buried beneath a ton of empty chip packets, dirty washing, and books. Flexible hours and no teachers, self-driven with no due dates.

At two am gravel rattled on her window, setting the dog barking. Leaning out, she hissed at Zane.

'Go away. Now. It's raining.'

He argued. She stonewalled. Watching him through a gap in the blinds, she saw him pull his hood over his head and sneak through the garden, sniffing and picking. As *if* he would have a clue. On the way out, he tossed a tattered poppy at her window and watched it fall back into the elderberry bushes

At three am rats squealed, scrabbled and fought above her head. Gross. The neighbour's front door banged, and Garnet rushed to the window, watching her mother slip in spitting rain across the yard, holding a black gar-bag over her head. Best kind of mother to come home shoeless from a feral neighbour's house at three am. Garnet heard her feet tap on the stairs.

'So, the bonfire?' In she came. Right into the bedroom. Dirty feet, breathless. 'Sorry to miss it.'

'Same every year.' Garnet sulked a bit and blew the shit out of four ferals on her old version of *Doom*.

'Saw your desk lamp on. Can't you sleep?'

'Why do you care?'

Raven reached for the brush on the dressing table and stood behind Garnet to make strong clean sweeps through her hair. 'Nine-point-three repeating.'

'You smell like an animal.'

'And you have grass in your hair. Shall I bring you a warm drink?'

'If you want. It would be different.'

'Have you been talking to the Zane boy online?' Raven probed.

'Don't call him that. You don't even know him.'

Raven shook out her hair and slid away. Probably too ashamed to ask if her daughter knew about protective behaviour, when she had set such an unsafe example.

Another time Raven had come to her room late at night, *high, high, high*. Garnet had pulled down weird tracks and they had danced around the room, shimmied and shrieked, dressed up and giggled, chorused like karaoke. Substance-enhanced relationships were the least complicated.

Raven pressed a wine glass of warm liquid onto her palm.

'What is it? Ratbane?'

'Tansy. Leaves and flowers strained and sweetened with honey. Raven prescribes it for rheumatic pains, digestive cramps and hysteria.'

'Who is this Raven woman?'

'Tell *me*. I want to know.'

'Poison, is it? Or a therapeutic dose?'

'Such an ingrate.'

No doubt about it, years ago, Raven would have been accused of witchcraft and rolled down the hill in a flaming tar barrel. Nothing had changed. Garnet proffered a small mean smile, sniffed and ducked her head into her glass. 'Do you have to visit next door?'

'How could I not like a man named Branwell after reading the Brontë sisters?'

'Wasn't he the evil brother who bullied them?'

'This Branwell was named by his English mother.'

'He looks Chilean or something.'

'Father from Columbia. Bit by bit, I'm gleaning his story.' She kissed Garnet's forehead. 'He split from his wife before she developed lupus. And still set her up for independent living, so he can't be all bad. Now that she can't work, it costs him a fortune.'

'Perhaps she'll get better.'

'I'm afraid not.'

'Why did he move here?'

'It's cheaper. Cash flow problems paying for care. I feel sorry for him.'

'Of course you do. Why can't you be normal?' Garnet blurted. 'You want to save everyone but me.'

'That's not true. What's going on?'

'I have to put up with a lot of shit at school because of you.'

'Oh?' Raven lit a cigarette, leaned back and folded her arms around her thin body.

'You've got this thing with men, I know. Even Zane's father. Aren't you too old to play doctor games?'

Raven started back. 'I made an error in judgement with Andrew. Harm none. Got out in time. No one's business but ours.' Then shrugged, stubbed out her cigarette in a cup and turned toward the window.

Garnet sniffed. 'Don't stand near the curtain. He'll think it's me.'

'You're smart to tune in to your personal radar.'

'Why are you doing this? If you lie down with dogs, you'll get up with fleas. No wonder my father left you. You pretend you don't like men, but you do. And where's Ebba's husband? Why are we women living alone?'

'He died.'

'How am I supposed to grow up normal if all the men in my life disappear? How am I supposed to work everything out when you can't? You're old.'

'Don't be cruel.' Tears welled in Raven's eyes. 'We never taught you that. Unconditional positive regard. Remember?'

Garnet raised her eyebrows and sniffed. 'I'll throw salt after you.'

'I'm just one person, and I'm doing my best? You also have Ebba. I'm sorry you don't feel supported.'

Garnet softened. 'I'm a bit tired. I feel funny about him living so close, when you and Ebba go to work.'

Her mother kissed the top of her head and fled. 'I understand.'

Ting

Garnet crawled across the room to grab her backpack. Her fingers seized on an abandoned lip balm, chewing gum, her leather wallet, a water bottle and a thick comb, one after the other, until she lost her temper and upended the bag onto the floor. The phone clattered out and she snatched it up. Shame, only Zane.

Outside come down
    U woke me
    Come anyway
    Go away Zane, I saw you snooping in our garden.
    R U sure?
    Get a life.

Was he a complete loser? Did he ever sleep?

Garnet tossed and turned; her fingers found and wound around the fringe on her quilt, and in the morning, she woke too early, felt wrecked again. When she went to check in on her mother, the bedclothes were cold to touch. Where had she gone now? Ebba snored on. The storm had blown through, the river rushed savagely after it, dumped debris on the banks and blew a strong earthy smell through the kitchen window. Little puffs of smoke. And black ash from their bonfire shifted in the chill breeze.

Across the driveway, the neighbour's door swung in the breeze. Carelessly left unlocked. After all, his car was missing. Garnet tiptoed softly past the dog, heart lurching, ready to retreat. She should keep walking. Not worry about her mother.

'Bark not,' she whispered, like a Goth princess. His tail thumped. Way out of character. Was he on something too? She risked a pat. Tomorrow she would feed him some of their overblown zucchinis. Maybe she would try harder with the man for her mother's sake. Maybe she would find her in danger inside and save her.

Inside the door, she hesitated. Listened. Noticed photographs splayed like a hand of cards across the wooden kitchen table.

Garnet by the river, pensive, knees drawn up.

Garnet climbing into Zane's car, chin defiant.

Garnet in the garden, lips locked against Zane's, body curved and languorous Not herself.

Savage hatred stirred inside her. He'd spied on her.

Tucked beneath, she saw photos of her mother, soft and floaty, a curtain of hair covering part of her face, a protective hand over her breasts, as she leaned back against chrome and leather gym apparatus. In another, completely naked, her hair streamed out behind her, as she strode joyously along the narrow river path. Nothing wrong with skyclad. Ebba and Raven believed nakedness healthy but...

Raven must have let him photograph *her*. Garnet fled, clattered through the door, home to her own cottage and up the stairs, to fling herself across her bed. The bastard had used a telephoto lens to capture her, the underaged daughter. How dare he? A good mother should have noticed his change of focus. Garnet had not consented.

Chapter Nine

STALEMATE: CANCELLATION

Film no. 5: kimmer@paisley.net.uk. Why did the films always arrive soon after Garnet gathered information? Sites where she registered... were they tracking her with cookies? Like surveillance? It was a thing now.

'best mare could miss a foal.mov' showed a riderless horse – signifying death?

Its neck and flanks foamed with exertion; its mane dirty and knotted. People coughed blood in a pathological way as if in the throes of consumption. Bells rang in Garnet's head. The sixteenth-century shawled girl, who gathered herbs and tended ill people, looked bruised, long-suffering. Witching times must have tangled up with the spread of tuberculosis.

If only she could splice the film clips together and make some sense of them. To prove they all connected with historical witchcraft. The fact that she had only seen each clip once had become her number one frustration. In the event she forgot them altogether, she had kept copious notes. Gaia knows how many films would arrive or what they meant. But it had become very clear that someone had noticed her interest in the subject and set her on a disturbing path.

. . .

On Tuesday, Garnet waited and watched her mother pick tansy leaves from the bed nearest the river, and then went straight back to her computer. The flowers looked like little yellow buttons and had 'an emmenagogue effect', which meant to bring on menstruation, even when not a period is not due. According to Wiki, drinking up to four cups a day of an infusion of flowers and leaves, the week before a period, stimulated a rush of blood.

Online, the emmenagogue crap was constant. Women always obsessed over late periods fearing they could be pregnant. Could a plant shift an unplanned baby? How often was it toxic? Bleeding was one thing, seizures and liver damage another. Women who healed with herbs, aka witches, hadn't deserved to die, but getting rid of babies would be a sticking point – perfect word choice. Where was the proof? The girls might have been miscarrying. Of course, authorities didn't bother much with proof in those days. They threw alleged witches in the river and if they sank, conceded their innocence. Bad luck – you lose – die a martyr.

Now, better ways to stop a baby were available – hard to access in small communities where doctors would not see girls without their mothers, but safer at least. With Ebba's work counselling teenagers about their reproductive health, Garnet felt no need to worry. And she didn't have a boyfriend. A baby at her age would be ridiculous.

She scooted downstairs for a snack and found Raven seated in her rocking chair nursing a mug of tea while she read. The tansy had not been intended for Garnet. Perhaps her mother wanted to sweat out a cold or fever. Garnet filed menst.doc. and scooted back to the witch trials.

It seemed that, as the professor she'd emailed had said, most accusations had been made in little places where small courts prevailed. Ordinary people became hysterical denouncers and accusations flew recklessly about. The highest numbers of trials had occurred in Scotland and Germany, where clergy dominated the courts and became experts at the game.

A John Kinkaid in Paisley had developed a reputation for his skill in picking witches. When his colleague the Reverend Blackwell left the ministry in 1694, surprise, surprise – no more witches were found.

Garnet remembered Reverend Hale in *The Crucible,* a witch expert who believed that *no crack in the fortress may be accounted small.* These men, seriously mad.

The Paisley and Salem narratives shared both style and content. Some historians believed that the witch-hunt in Salem influenced the outbreak of accusations in Paisley, because the clergy knew about those trials. Encouraging local grievances took people's minds off low wages, bad working conditions, and other forms of injustice. Shortly before the trials, pamphlets forbidding witchcraft had been published and distributed. Perhaps they gave someone an idea. Surely not a little girl like Christian, though.

Praise Gaia, this should never happen again. While she adored Cody, she worried about her ferrying confidences between her Zonta-going mother and Garnet's female household. Of course, Cody would never deliberately seek to hurt her, but what if in her frustrations over student life, she got in a muddle and got details wrong and shared them with judgy people who believed in 'one available truth, in this world and the next.' Where had she read that?

Ebba and Raven could be thrown in the river, tried by the service clubs and hung in front of the drive-through bottle shop. Garnet could be next. She would need to remind Cody over and over. That even seemingly well-meaning people in small towns could cause harm.

ALMOST APRIL

Hard to believe that Garnet's wheels had fallen off in English. Sure, she had seriously forgotten the due date for the exercise on Scene 1 in *The Crucible*, which she could have done with her hands tied behind her back and not inhaled. A bad hair day as well. Before she got to class, she looked a sleep-deprived wreck. Mr Drake had crashed his hard drive and sabotaged his own motherboard.

Stuff it, since when had ten-centimetre holes in tights violated the uniform code? Of course, Garnet knew he was really annoyed about her failure to submit the assignment because she was the only student who had showed an interest in the play.

After she ran through the standard spiel in the front office and accepted punishment number forty-five – tong duty on the oval – and presented back at the classroom, the teacher had left the room and no joke, her class members were throwing food, Cody in the thick of it. On return, Drako went apeshit. Then the fullback for the football A's, whose name would never pass Garnet's lips, put his hand on her bum, moved his fingers north and said, 'Honk if you want a bonk.'

Garnet's 'sometime friends' screeched, 'Scritch if you hear a witch,' and she stacked it, first dropping her rubbish bag near the bin, then marched out the door. Scuff-toed, snotty-nosed, bawling, she ran across the oval.

Cody dogged her tracks. 'Hey, babe.'

'I'll call you tonight.'

Lyndon turned up next, as if he'd already heard.

'Piss off! Please.'

Garnet had never walked all the way home. Fifteen kilometres felt like a marathon. Entering the driveway from the main road, she remembered her new feeling of imprisonment in her *own* home. Under surveillance. Now? Bent double, she crept past his car on the other side of the hedge and hoped he wouldn't spot her with his damned telephoto lens. The dog loosed a low blood-curdling growl. Visualising a row of toothmarks on her leg, she suppressed an anguished cry, as she scurried down the side of the house for spare keys beneath a pot and slid inside.

The shower had always been the best place to have a decent howl. Warm water washed off tears, and music made it possible to fool your low mood. Soon the bathroom turned fuggy with steam and soap and sweat. Cross-legged on the floor of the shower, Garnet examined her blisters for a long time, until the hot water ran out. She kind of hoped no one else needed water to amend their tough day. Bad luck, Ebba and Raven.

Towel around her shoulders, she turned off the taps, remained seated and moped. Overtired. Overwrought. That's what Ebba would say. School reports for ten years had documented Garnet's vivid imagination and her intermittent lack of interest. She rose and stared into the cloudy mirror.

Suddenly, her hearing became acute: honeyeaters, the next-door dog barking, insect scrapings, and tree branches dancing on the bevelled glass louvres. Out of present time the air cooled around her, as if comforting family had slid away. Fingers of ice slammed through the bathroom door. Garnet's heart leapt. Stop crying. She stuffed the end of her towel hard into her mouth and gagged. Someone must be out there? High-pitched eldritch laughter erupted — in her head? Ask anyone, she could conjure vividness. Loud parrots skimmed past the top louvre, and she tightened the towel around her body. Stay calm, stay calm. Her mouth trembled in front of the vanity mirror.

Crosshatched with her wan reflection, arms curled around his thin torso, the boy appeared. Filaments of moisture shone in his tight, tiny curls. Always, always, when she felt most upset, he materialised. Light must have refracted through the bevelled glass, created a doubling effect, and she took some stupid comfort from it, as she squinted into the sunrays beaming through the window. Until her vision returned to normal and only her own reflection remained, she would hold her breath. Her rational brain pooh-poohed stuff she'd read about doppel-gangers.

Light-headed and full of déjà vu, her lips tingled, her fingers twitched with pins and needles. Had she turned into her mother? Seeing things. She took steady breaths. Slowly, the boy, dissolved in the steamy room, faded away. Garnet leant back against the shower wall, panting with relief. What she heard next, restarted her heart, louder than a lawnmower.

Gravel crunched again on the path below the bathroom window. Heavy boots moved steadily past the wall towards the sunroom door. Had Ebba even locked it? No point thinking about Raven, who felt ambivalent about life itself. Keeping herself or anyone safe would never get a guernsey. Was the menace real? Was *he* in the house?

Someone tapped on the door and called out. 'Garnet, are you alright?'

'Don't come in,' she screeched and stepped forward to slide the metal bolt across the bathroom door.

Bloody him. Gaia, such nerve. Garnet quaked, behind the door. Terror rose like vomit in her throat. 'Go away.' Likely, he wanted to bite her again, like one of his damned birds. After she dialled 000, she would scratch his eyes out. Any heavy breathing belonged to her.

After what seemed a very long time, she heard the person leave her house. Heard a car start in the driveway. She flew out of the bathroom and checked locks on doors and windows — too late – but somehow it comforted her.

For the rest of the afternoon, she tried not to freak out. Drew her curtains. Stayed upstairs. Played *Zelda*. An old RPG, but she still liked it. It made her feel like a kid again. More herself. She leapt into the story, shooting, running, and killing. Then took herself offline to doze until dusk. A heap of messages lay in wait.

Ting

Cody: Unbelievable. Teacher with bum hanging out of pants sucks to cause you all that grief.

Garnet: I'm over it. Almost.

Cody: Wish you'd let me come home with you.

Garnet: Hey, I was way too foul for company.

Cody: big hugs.

Garnet: I need to talk to you soon.

Lyndon: Are you okay? Did you really walk home? FWIW that was fucking sad.

Garnet: walk did me good. Blew a whole heap of stuff out before I got home. TTYL

Lyndon: S

Zane: Quite an exit.

Garnet: No fair.

Zane: beaver on, girl.

Garnet: screaming.

Kendra: Daisy with me. Worried about you? Forget what happened. Everyone else has.

Garnet: Hi to Daisy too. Went into overload. Tired. Talk later.

At six o'clock, her mother drove in and, after a few minutes, called her name. Located her upstairs. 'Garnet, the school called.'

'More to the point, Raven, your dropkick boyfriend tried to bust me in the shower today.'

'So he said.'

'He *told* you?'

'Said he heard noises. Knew we were all at work and school and thought he'd better check.'

'Do you believe him?'

'No reason not to. Is there...?'

'Whatever, Raven, whatever. He scared me witless tapping on the bathroom door, but he didn't break it down and ravish me, so what can I say?'

'Why were you home?'

'Felt disgusting.'

'And how did you get home?'

'Walked. Left in a hurry.'

'Fifteen kilometres.' Her expression seemed tender. 'Garnet, I have degrees in jigging school. What's wrong?'

Garnet stared at her bleakly. Raven still wanted to play the mother card and why not? It challenged her, but today she looked fit enough. In fact, she'd been up with a capital 'U' for weeks: healthy, full of vim; just a few dark lines under her eyes; her voice regaining a certain brittle quality. Sometimes, it happened that way.

Did it matter that Raven had cavorted naked along the riverside, stayed out all night with a man diametrically opposed to her attitudes and values, and that she still wanted to dispense advice? She would save Branwell's photography for later. Garnet cleared her throat and tried not to cry. 'Well, I'm getting flak at school. They're dumping on you and Ebba again.'

'What are they saying this time?'

'Nothing much... really. Muscle-flexing. Crap about witches. Uniform code.'

'I'll go down there. I'll sort out that testosterone-challenged little Principal again.'

'Don't bother. I'm handling it.'

'But not today?' Raven gently touched her daughter's cheek.

'I've been tired. I forgot to get an assignment in.'

'So...' Raven twirled her finger through her hair.
'Don't worry about it. I'm chilled now.'
'You'll go to school tomorrow?'
She nodded. 'I'm not a quitter, Raven.'
'That's my girl.'

Garnet found Ebba lying down in her bedroom and snuggled in. 'Ask not, Ebba. Rave on, not Raven to me.'

Ebba told her about a Scottish wizard who tried to make a young girl fall in love with him by making a charm with three of her pubic hairs. How abhorrent. Perhaps he gathered them from her bathroom. When someone substituted three hairs from a cow's udder, a love-struck cow followed him all over town. Ebba's fingers soothed Garnet's hair.

'I have good feelings about you,' Ebba whispered, and Garnet felt grateful.

Grey Card. It seemed the school required some sort of re-entry. A Red Card led Garnet straight back to the front office. So, she had nicked school. What were they going to do, suspend her? The principal could tell her where to sit, what to wear, what to read, how to think and who to be. *Sure. Anything.* He steepled his fingers and asked a lot of questions about things that were none of his business and insisted on her booking a session with the school counsellor. She submitted because she had no other options. Hummed until the counsellor collected her. They must just have thought she'd make another break for it.

'Garnet, you're not taking me seriously.'
'Ms C. I am, I am!' She ducked her head.
'Tell me, what's wrong? Are you depressed, anorexic, pregnant? Is this a harassment issue?'
Select 'd'. Like the biology exam.
Yeah, but don't worry about it. I know you can't do anything about it. She was the mother of the football player who had ... for fuck's sake.

'Garnet, think again. Was there anything you wish you'd done differently? Girls need to be assertive but also intelligent. Were you manifesting any victim-like behaviour?'

'Yeah, I was. Trying to attract attention.' Beneath her skirt, Garnet dug her fingernails into her leg.

'Would it help, dear, if you told me who harassed you? We could initiate some group work. Team building exercises. Role-play with the other person.' The counsellor leaned towards her. 'Restorative justice.'

Garnet thought about this. She could go to their place for dinner. The husband could have a go at her too.

'No really, Mrs C., It's cool. I'm fine. I just had a bad day.'

'Very well. If you change your mind, please do come and avail yourself of my support.' If the counsellor had tied her tubes sixteen years ago, maybe that would have been helpful. Then Garnet wouldn't have had to deal with her son.

Cody caught up with her in second maths. She looked pale and unwell, her eyes bloodshot, her uniform oddly grotty. Garnet decided not to rock her boat about the witch business. She felt too tired to think up the right questions anyway. They hugged. Everyone else, she withered at ten paces with her scowl. Maybe she should leave the school. Enrol at a different one. She could drive to the city with Ebba.

Squeezed between the slats of her locker she found a note from Lyndon:

Can we get together? What are you doing tomorrow? Email me tonight, just yes or no. L

Ting

    Garnet: I'm a bit freaked out right now. What do you want?

    Lyndon: I want to talk to you. Can I come over tomorrow?

    Garnet: Early. I'm going to the market to help Raven.

    Lyndon: Can I come too?

Garnet: Alright.

She sounded pathetic, but she didn't want to entertain him alone at home either. Ebba was going to the city to facilitate a weekend workshop titled 'The Damaged Psyche –Making Feminism Work for You.' Seriously…

Lyndon: What time?

Garnet: Early – 8.30. I suppose it won't matter. No one will see us out there.

Lyndon: Pass me the poisoned chalice. What have I done?

Garnet: Nothing. I'm just being a bitch. Sorry.

She sprawled across her bed and scoffed down organic chocolate while she flicked through computer mags. Choices at the newsagent had shrunk to almost nothing. She should organise a subscription online.

Perhaps she had PMS. Boys slagged off at school about 'moody girls' and it continually offended her. In the late seventeenth century, men thought women strange and mysterious – messy – with their bleeding and their birthing. It made them terrified. She could make Lyndon afraid of her tomorrow if she bothered.

Ting

Film clip, no. 6: 'two or three nights.mov'.

Garnet had given up trying to save them. She ran it through. Saw young men drag the same girl from her dwelling. Only the backs of their coats visible, their heads above the frame. When the girl began to shout, something about being of good heart, they cried *witch* and spat into her face, before the video buffered. Several faces morphed over the girl's – her features had never been clear. The filmmaker must have wanted this effect.

Garnet got up and kicked an empty drink can into the curtains.

Queer things were happening, but she shouldn't count the emails. In the face of maternal mayhem, she prided herself on being a hard rationalist. Someone knew about her interest in Scottish witchcraft. That was all.

No way it would be the aunt in Paisley. Not even to interest Garnet in family history. Who would go to so much trouble? Had one of her lovely friends embedded a worm in an email, to report on her witchy cruising? Administrators could look at anything on their network, even email. It had to be simpler than that. Surely the person who had sent the marching cats had accessed her folders.

Tomorrow she would ask Lyndon. She read the rest of an article, and then played with key words, anything she could think of related to kimmer and paisley. Still a brick wall.

Chapter Eleven

MOON: NURTURING

As Raven backed Ebba's four-wheeled-drive out onto the main road, Lyndon appeared, hat pulled down, backpack at the ready, headphones plugged into his lugs. He chained his bike inside the gate and got in the car.

Garnet shimmied over to make room for him. Raven had stuffed the back of the four-wheel-drive with pots of herbs. This early in the morning, no one said much. Raven drove like a maniac, twitched the steering wheel back and forth with two fingers, flirted with large river gums protected on the bends by guard rails. Lyndon had driven around with Zane, so presumably, no parental consent required. Raven raved, all the way to the valley community hall. Every now and then, she beamed over Garnet's head at Lyndon. Presumably, she wanted him to like her.

When Garnet was little, she had liked the ordinariness of the market scene. Kids ran amongst the farm trucks, eating free oranges from the Riverland, and playing chasey amongst the pot plants. If they weren't acting too crazy, the organisers allowed them to sit at the Devonshire Tea tables and drink orange cordial out of old Vegemite glasses. Handcraft and produce tables lined the walls. She had coveted embroidered windcheaters, country cross-stitch for her bedroom, and cheap home-glued jewellery.

By the age of six, she had gotten used to minding the little rows of pots and bunches of herbs while her mother skipped down the river for a drag with the pottery hippy from James Track. The reactions of the other stallholders, when her mother wafted out of the hall in her floating arrangements of silk scarves, her layers of colour and texture, had not troubled her then. *Yatter, yatter, blitter, blitter*, talking about you, Garnet, poor little thing; talking about your mother too. *Isn't she gorgeous; pity she doesn't charge more for those herbs and give everyone a chance to make some money.* It took years to become a local, fifty at least, but probably if a tourist slagged on Raven, they would have flown to her defence.

While Raven set up her stall, Garnet and Lyndon bunked down in the back of the four-wheel-drive with a Styrofoam cup of instant coffee each and a handful of buttered scones.

Lyndon leaned against her side and chomped on his scone. A small bunger glowed like a beacon on his chin, and he had missed a tiny triangle of blonde bristles when shaving his chin. But he was pretty for a guy, with his long eyelashes, his body the right kind of thin. The air felt crisp and country-clean. It felt cosy sipping coffee together, blowing steam into the air, and staring at the action around them. Lyndon edged up on one buttock to walk his fingers to the bottom of his jeans pocket from where he drew a pack of chewing gum.

Garnet decided to spill her guts about the kimmer emails.

'Awesome or what?'

'I wish I could see the clips.'

'They've disappeared, remember.'

'I know, I know.'

'If you have any brilliant ideas about who sent them, why, and how, I'm up for it. All ears.' She pushed a strand of hair behind her ears. Then remembered that he had arranged their meeting. 'What did you want to talk to *me* about?'

'Cody's really wired lately. Have you noticed?'

'Well yes, but I haven't given it my full attention. Has she been talking about it with you?' Garnet felt a spasm of guilt, or was it jealousy? Yesterday, in general science, she had pulled her friend away from the Bunsen burner burning her plait. It had made a terrible stink.

'A bit. Judging by her emails there's not much happening in the sleep department. She needs to calm down.'

'I'll message her when I get home and see if she wants to come over tonight.'

'Good. Zane's frozen her out for some reason and she's not happy about that.'

'Zane?'

'Yeah. She won't tell me details.'

'Ask *him*.'

'I tried. He gives me that "talk to the hand because the face ain't listening" crap.'

'What a piece of work.'

'Zane's father knocks him round, you know.'

'I know. And he's a doctor. I've seen the bruises.'

Lyndon shrugged and slung an arm around her shoulders. 'I've got the weekend paper in my backpack. I nicked it at a farmer's gate. *He* won't enjoy his brown egg this morning. You want to toss for the funnies? Read the chess column?'

'Stealing. That's so not you. The world as I know it is falling apart.'

Raven looked too excitable when she descended upon them, danced up and down on the spot, laughed too-loudly, and swung her purple skirt above her brown knees. Would they cover her stall? The hippy looked stoned as he wobbled down the riverbank with her, wearing zodiac jewellery over his leather waistcoat and a pair of air-conditioned jeans that sagged low on his bum. Garnet liked his kind bearded face, soft-lined where smiles had been. Since she was six, he had aged a lot. So much for a natural diet, including weed.

Every market day, while she absentmindedly tried to sell herbs and other produce, Garnet chatted to old Mr Chevalier, who sold goat cheese at the trestle table next to her mother's. He'd promised an introduction to his brother's family in Normandy if Garnet ever took a gap year.

'Bonjour, Mademoiselle.' He nodded at Lyndon. 'How is cyberspace?'

'Sometimes it's the nicest world I know.' She smiled back.

'So true.' He winked. 'I have a proposition for you.'

'How very French.'

'An old man would have to toss and turn for nights to dream up a scheme to interest you.'

Lyndon laughed.

'Ho, so run it past me,' Garnet said, intrigued.

'You know that I am very successful with the cheese. I supply now many restaurants. I want to make a website about my business. Could you do this for me?'

'Of course. And if you get online, you can talk to your brother in France and organise my visit.'

'Wonderful,' he said, beaming. 'We will get together you and I, after they deliver my new computer? Do you have a website?'

'I've started building one.'

'Good. Garnet, here, take some of my chevron, slice it into thirds crossways, grill it on some bread. Serve it with some of your mother's beautiful 'erbs and just a little vinaigrette. *Magnifique*. Deposit on our partnership.'

'Thank you, Monsieur.'

'Chevron is cheese,' she whispered to Lyndon.

He grinned. 'I know you think that guys are not highly evolved, but steady on.'

Garnet patted his arm.

When Raven returned wearing an idiotic grin and the hippy's hat, Garnet and Lyndon sloped back to the car to finish reading the newspaper. The front-page news must be stale but Garnet liked the glossy mags in the middle. A strange feeling of contentment crept up on her, the sun warming her back, sitting next to an uncomplicated boy who laughed at her jokes and leaned against her. Cody and Zane would have to wait.

Home at three, they hugged by the gate, before Lyndon peddled away down the road.

'Take the paper back to the farmer,' she yelled after him.

He waved. 'Okay, okay. Talk later.'

Garnet scurried upstairs. She scanned a photo Ebba had taken of her in the garden, in which she wore hipster denims and a tight old Nike top.

She pinched and stretched the image until her messy hair and face filled the screen. Her mother's intense blue eyes stared back. The resemblance horrified her. She crosshatched her image against a photo she'd once snatched of the little boy in the mirror, expected nothing to appear, but to her surprise a blurry outline resolved and then dissolved.

Could she link the little boy or the girl in the vid to her Scottish peeps? Too fanciful? Very few people knew about her family link with Paisley. Only Ebba, Raven and, Gaia help her, if *she'd* told the neighbour anything so personal... Cody opened her mouth to change gears but surely would not blab about her closest friend; Zane hammered up mysteries and would be capable of it. And Lyndon? Some of the others might know vague details. John Proctor in the Crucible would *'nought'* blab like this: *'I speak for my own sins; I cannot judge another...I have no tongue for it.'*

Munching on a cold veggie burger, she messaged Cody.

Garnet: Hey chickee.
　　Cody: chickee sounds offensive?
　　Garnet: Ebba says some feminists reclaim the word. Do you feel like visiting tonight? Siciliana Spaghetti — it's happening.
　　Cody: Maybe. I'm feeling flat. Lyn's been on my case all morning. Then she felt bad about nagging and gave me money. I went to the tattoo parlour.
　　Garnet: Incorrigible and no ID, huh. Did you get a tat?
　　Cody: Just a tongue stud.
　　Garnet: How much did it hurt?
　　Cody: Quite a bit. Shop has an autoclave so I'm clean at least. They put in an extra-long stud to allow for swelling.
　　Garnet: I guess that's the end of your career as a speech therapist.
　　Cody: I'm in my room so Lyn and Gord won't notice I'm lisping. Sucking ice. Should settle soon. Zane wants to go out tonight.
　　Garnet: Message me later when you've worked out your best option.

Cody: Zane and I have got something to sort but I'd rather come and see you.

Garnet tried not to feel annoyed. What did she care about Zane and Cody sorting issues? But when she thought about it, she did. What if they'd been dumping on Ebba and Raven again? What if they were causing her problems?

Yet some days she hated Raven. Without any idea of the shit her daughter went through, her mother made things worse. Shortly after she sent her daughter next-door bearing sage and marjoram, Garnet made the decision to give Lyndon a hard copy of all the notes on her film clips. She had to trust someone; Ebba hadn't kept up with tech, but then who could?

Garnet knew exactly why Raven had sent her. It had been a lesson, whereby she was supposed to feel shame that she had so misunderstood a straightforward, adult man who had shown genuine neighbourly concern for her safety. No real sympathy for why Garnet had jigged school. No sense of neighbourly boundaries.

The man called her from the depths of the house where she found him perched on a ladder painting out a bedroom. The ceiling paint bled wetly into the walls.

'Hi,' he said. Smiling, urbane. Red cheek outlines glistened on the black painted cement floor. He wouldn't do that — press his backside against wet paint, would he?

'Do you like my work? It's supposed to be mad and menstrual,' he said.

Yes, he *would*. Definitely. His voice sounded as well-moderated, as if he'd said 'it's pastoral — atonal — conveys the warm autumn chaos of the valley.'

'Do you think you should speak to me like that?' Garnet felt forced into an unfamiliar, conservative position. Backing away through the bedroom door, she abandoned the bunch of sage upon a coffee table as she passed. Magazines – rude European ones – lay open. She moved the bunch of herbs to cover one of the women.

'Would you like to paint a spider in the corner?' he called after her. 'This could be our reconciliation project.'

At the door, she turned back to look at him, where he remained balanced on the bottom rung of the ladder, paintbrush dangling from his left hand. 'Jesus, you sound like Mr Rochester. You even speak like him.' She thought she might choke.

He sprang off the ladder and moved toward her, one of his eyebrows feigning puzzlement. 'I'm only teasing. I don't know many teenagers.'

'I'm sorry about your wife?'

'Yes, I expect your mother told you, a challenging prognosis. Stay a while. I'll get you a drink – an orange juice?'

'No, I have to go.'

He shrugged and smiled. 'Next time perhaps.'

She moved down the narrow passageway, feeling his hand between her shoulder blades as he guided her forward. A lot of men did that. It didn't mean anything sinister. All the same, she felt confused. Was she jealous that he snaffled more time with her mother than she did? Liquid bubbled in pans on the stove. When he stepped away then, to turn down the gas, she flew out, banging the door behind her, leapt at the last minute over another message on the step.

Raven had no shame. No doubt *he* would use the herbs to make sage butter and blend it into his pasta sauce; or worse, disembowel a poor bloody bird and stuff it with sage dressing. How could such a man attract her mostly vegetarian mother? And Ebba – surely, she must see the man's behaviour as much more than eccentricity.

Garnet kicked the stones across the path. Men made *her* awkward. Was it them or her?

Her mother worked among rows of fading opium poppies, deep in the garden, but looked up when the screen door slammed. To calm down, Garnet stooped to examine chives flowering madly by the tap. Affecting nonchalance, she held the buds in her fingers, surprised by the gauzy fineness, as soft and strong as pantihose. Touched the tiny white flowers, folded one in against the other, ready to tear through the silky bag and open into the sun. When she looked up again her mother had disappeared.

Inside the warm and fuggy house, Garnet fingered late blooming summer flowers in bowls. Yellow pollen stained the wooden furniture and damp petal piles mounted. She shut down the fire and drank rainwater. Raven had filled her Moses baskets with her riverside gatherings and stacked them in the hallway. Almost straightaway, she came inside, holding paper envelopes full of poppy seeds. Garnet thought she looked overripe, flushed like the poppies, when she gushed about seeding another bed, then changed tack.

'Ignore her until you feel better,' Garnet schooled herself.

'Did the neighbour eat your tongue instead of the sage?'

Not far off the truth. She would not talk to her about him. 'You're not even close.'

What kind of parent would send a kid in there? No matter how carefully Garnet observed her mother, she never caught the actual moment of change, when everyday oddness turned to discord. Raven prickled, set her hands on her hips. Cornered, she might shout. Everything she did would fall out of sync.

'You know that teasing is a kind of bullying,' Garnet added.

Now Raven looked awkward and reached for a jug of homebrew.

'What are you drinking?'

'Absinthe. Branwell made it for me.'

Garnet wanted to say, *Mother, it's not even five pm and you're drinking wormwood. Get a grip.* 'Never ask me to go next door again.'

Her mother protected the jug with her arm.

'If you do, I will bring a pointy reckoning that will shudder you.'

Quite suddenly, she felt mean, and moved towards Raven. Tears? Surely not tears. She pressed her lips against her mother's forehead.

Upstairs another film awaited Garnet: 'ye hae a puir mean speerit.mov'

They were coming in thick and fast now. Someone seriously wanted to freak her out. In this one, two people sat at a simple deal table. A small stream of others, mostly females, passed by in front of them. The setting lacked clarity, perhaps a church or just a freestone wall. A young man in a big hat and wearing a black mask read from a list.

Dour, he looked, and vaguely familiar – but also barely real, most of his face covered by the fleshy mask tucked into his clerical collar. Nor could the girl be easily viewed, from behind or in profile. Clips always sped too fast for identification. A lumpy, hunched-over woman sat beside the minister, dowdy bonnet obscuring her face. When she stamped on his foot beneath the table, he scribbled a name with his feather quill.

Garnet knew exactly what the clip depicted. Recognised the set up from an article she'd saved in her Paisley folder. The girl had been accused and brought to court. The plump woman stamped on the minister's foot to identify the accused, whose names he recorded. The girl would be interrogated and tried for witchcraft. Had it been the same with Christian Shaw, or had they made allowances for her youth? Had she been allowed to whisper in the minister's ear in the privacy of her nursery?

Garnet watched the clip carefully before it disappeared, then took her usual notes. For a few minutes, as she gathered her thoughts, she lay on her bed listening to Kate Bush and Enya on Ebba's Walkman. Womany stuff, way out of date. What had Lyndon said about power being local and unstable? Little places or any places could be a problem?

Last year Ebba had made a pilgrimage in southern India. Ironic, that she had purchased something high-tech to record her experiences, which she hadn't used since. It had been tacit that Garnet would gain custody of the fancy camera on Ebba's return – far more satisfactory than a tea towel, a t-shirt or a jewel-coloured sari. Garnet hauled it out and began to fiddle, played with its effects, changed photos from colour to sepia, planned a short video. Leaning out her window, she recorded Raven, cutting and trimming as she moved through the garden.

'Could you work for a moment with Ebba's shawl over your head instead of around your hips?' she called. Raven readily assented. Garnet recorded and played it back.

'What are you doing?' her mother called up to her.

'Experiments.'

At a distance, the effect was comparable to the Paisley clips. The landscape indistinct and grainy but evocative. Maximised, it looked quite like the clips. Raven looked like a crone. The sound was fuzzy, and in fact, quite unclear. It felt like a breakthrough.

The backgrounds in the film clips looked European, but any corner of an old-fashioned garden would do the trick. Had she been able to replay and pause the videos every second, she might have found more clues. Now the clips would sink into the deep web. Three new search engines later, she hit the second jackpot – a Paisley service provider. She copied and pasted an email contact and wrote:

Are you aware of another Scottish internet provider – named Kimmer? Please send me a price schedule re internet access. Do you charge monthly or have any current deals? Would prefer credit card transaction. Can other clients access my address without my consent?
Sincerely, Garnet Southwood

How easy would payment be if she used Ebba's Visa card. Raven had been forbidden access, when unwell anyway. Ebba was bloody sick of bailing her daughter out of court and library fines, parking and speeding fines, and a lot of final notices for bills as well. When she first fell ill, Raven couldn't organise her way out of a paper bag. If under eighteen, the filmmaker would have needed access to an adult credit card. That would be dead easy with a normal parent, busy as hell, skimming their Bankcard statements. They'd pay up without even checking items.

Garnet continued to play with the camera while she waited for the Paisley provider to respond. Perhaps they were asleep right now. She checked the time difference – about twelve hours. Cody hadn't got back to her either. And there were so many other things to think about – the beastly neighbour, family harassment, the films, Zane – she must not lose her grip. Even though she had no science in which to frame him, the benign little boy had never really frightened her.

Ebba slid a plate of thyme and butternut gnocchi under her nose and tiptoed away. At ten pm Garnet lay on her bed half-dreaming. Pieces of all the puzzles must be hidden in her hard drive. Demonic cats and film clips had marched into her life and seemed to be taking over. It felt like a violation.

Ting

 Dear Ms Southwood,

 Thank you for your enquiry. I am unaware of an internet company named Kimmer. I believe you'll find us competitive.

 Attached, you will find fee structures and protocol for Paisley Online. Payment is usually made by credit card. Encryption ensures security. Please read our FAQ, if you have any concerns, submit your credit number over two e-mails to avoid any concern about data leaks.

 Disclosing details of our client's email addresses would breach confidentiality. I am sure you will find this reassuring. Please feel free to contact us with any further questions.

 Sincerely, blah, blah...

Yes. It would be dead easy. She chewed the skin around her fingernails. At midnight, visitors arrived next door. Garnet peered through the curtains at a tall man and a thin blonde girl, both wearing black leather jackets. They ferried cardboard boxes into a Range Rover. It seemed Branwell traded more than birds. The man shook hands with him, tugged at the girl's coat and climbed back in the car, hurriedly reversing along the driveway to the main road.

Quite suddenly, a caged bird shrieked, and the neighbour looked up at her window. Garnet shrank back. She pulled down three thrash tracks and let them rip. *Bloody, bloody, bloody.* Then opened her major essay on *The Crucible,* due at the end of the week. She didn't want to cross swords with Drako again, especially after the late minor assignment. Not so long ago, she has been his pet nerd. What had he said about the girls and mass clinical hysteria? Head close to the screen, she pulled on headphones and started editing her rough draft. She would put the neighbour from her mind.

*The people of Salem, near Boston New England, and those of 16c Pais-
ley, Scotland lived in difficult times. In both historical spaces, the church
tried to stamp out evil but, despite their stern efforts, evil walked right in,
infecting brothers, sisters, mothers, fathers, like a plague. Evil that over
four weeks in the Salem summer of 1642, hung nineteen people for practising witchcraft. In 1697, seventeen people were condemned to be
burned at the stake, on Paisley's Gallows Green.*

Ebba had told Garnet about an article in *The Washington Post*
which speculated about what had ailed the girl accusers in Salem: the
true story shaped into a play by Arthur Miller. Their symptoms resem-
bled those of bad acid trips, but likely a result of eating rye bread conta-
minated with ergot, the fungus from which LSD was derived. Perhaps
one had suffered a genuine episode and play-acted from then on.
Between fits, Christian Shaw had also seemed perfectly well. During her
seizures, witnesses claimed, she went stiff and threw her head about.
Afterwards, she apparently became deaf and blind yet giggled when they
read from the scriptures.

Garnet wondered whether Christian Shaw had suffered infantile
convulsions. She had had one herself at the age of four, brought about
by a high temperature. But surely historians would have thought of that.

The essay had grown to over a thousand words, and she hadn't yet
written a conclusion. Without cuts, Drako would mark her down for
busting the word limit. Garnet yawned and stretched. All she'd done
tonight was stress about the film clips and a small amount of English
homework. When she peeked outside, the neighbour's cottage lay once
more in darkness.

At two am another film arrived. Garnet sat up in fright. They were
coming steadily now. She had heard that mass murderers always turned
up the heat near the end, either to unhinge people or to feed their own
bloodlust.

She shivered and opened 'Exodus XX11, 18 .mov' from kimmer@
paisley.com.uk, then googled the verse: 'Thou shalt not suffer a witch to
live.'

Very Christian. Not. This time the girl lay sprawled across a flag-
stone floor. Someone swung a lantern near her face, making her throw

up her hands as if warding off a blow. Back turned to the camera, robed figures dragged her to her feet. The girl's hands covered her face, and the footage turned blurrier. In the dying moments of the film, she collapsed upon the floor.

Garnet knew immediately what had happened. The clips began to make more and more sense. The Scots had chosen sleep deprivation to torture confessions of guilt from accused witches. Day after day, they kept the victim awake, threatening and awakening her continually until she became disoriented. By then, she would agree to anything, if they would only let her rest.

If they continually woke and watched the alleged witches, no one could criticise their treatment. What could be more reasonable? As a bonus, it often led to more accusations. Some posts suggested that the Scots had invented this effective form of torture, continued to this day. Honest volunteers worked in shifts, to watch the witch, who lay either in shameful disarray or drab in sackcloth before them, until her hallucinations had begun.

For a moment, Garnet let her imagination take rein. Maybe she had touched some chord from the past – perhaps she had a gift that neither Ebba nor Raven knew about – and had unleashed a restless spirit. Was it because someone had followed her online or because she was receptive, available, and a good medium?

She knew that she was kidding herself. Spirits unleashed visions, catastrophic natural events, or prophetic signs. They didn't inhabit computers.

But there had been a loose correlation between the films and the whispers at school. Garnet had once been inured to gossip and to social conformity. *Anyone could make friends*; she had always told herself that. Ebba, working in the city, tended to bother less about knowing people. The cottage became her sanctuary because she valued peace, privacy. Raven had made more relationships, albeit some unsuitable. That was her way, to gulp at life, tasting, taking, never finding true happiness. Poor mother. The film clips had started to add up and Garnet felt uneasy. Mystery or malice. Neither choice palatable.

Chapter Twelve

DISCORD: LOSS

Outside, darkness deepened... The boy's face appeared, as familiar as the rest of the room reflected in her window. Sudden gunshots exploded across the river, shattering her reverie. Birds shrieked across the sky. Garnet turned her desk lamp off and ran to throw up the sash and locate the hunters. She shivered. Ebba would say a goose had walked over her grave.

Lights bounced along the riverbank. Spotlighters, perhaps, on the back of a truck roaring across the paddocks. Soon, she would hear more shots. Bullets would tear into animal flesh. A memory of the neighbour's rifle triggered more: him following her mother along the riverbank, or stalking game under the trees. Did he shoot his birds? Almost certainly. Unless bullets spoiled the meat. The world seemed full of violence.

The urge to run surged through her veins, heaved through her lungs, seized up her brain. Ghosts unleashed in Paisley two hundred years ago rushed down the line towards her. To dispel them, she rested her head against the window recess and took deep, deliberate breaths.

A north wind whipped the trees and pushed smoke along the valley. A sulphury haze wreathed the moon. Dirty gunmetal-coloured clouds splotched the sky. Stars brightened in-between spaces. Dust whirled through the poison garden, where Garnet could see Ebba on her knees, planting in the moonlight. Probably praying to some female deity for a cleansing rain and unconcerned about the regular racket made by spot-lighters. Then she disappeared from sight.

Garnet tracked a plume of smoke to a clearing several hundred metres past Branwell's bottom fence line, where she saw a fire toss flames high into a gum tree. Farmers burnt off in autumn, too, and it had been a good season with plenty of growth. A few days ago, some of them had lit a bonfire on the hillside. But flickering figures arrested her attention as they moved beyond the trees – the neighbour and some drunken friends? Raven high on something, dancing round the fire, shrieking through the silver tussocks, running by the river?

Ebba reappeared near the bottom gate, white hair flying out behind her head, face tired and haggard, as she tromped up the path in men's track pants and heavy boots. When she caught Garnet's face at the upstairs window, she waved her trowel and called out.

'Bloody idiot kids. Did you see them? At least three, running behind the trees overhanging the rapids,' Ebba called.

'Kids. I heard shots.'

'I heard them too. Let's hope just neighbours spotting up by the waterfall track.'

'Come inside, it's late.'

'I think those boys walked in from the orchard and along the river. I've got a good mind to ring the police.'

'The fire won't go anywhere, Ebba. It's too damp. Look, it's quietening down already.'

Ebba nodded. 'I think they've gone. I heard a car revving. I'll go to bed.'

Ebba locked the back door and turned off outside lights before she came upstairs. Garnet needed earthing. She rotated her head into the camera lens and captioned it for her journal: *Possibly unhinged.*

Ting
　　Zane: Bewdiful night
　　Fire

Car on the corner
Garnet: You lit the fire, dickhead.
Zane: Come down.
Garnet: Busy. Go home.

Zane, building fires, running by the water. Must be trying to get at her, to light a fire so close to where she lived. Surely not Lyndon as well? On such a weird night, might any human company lift her spirits? Why go back to bed and court more nightmares? She turned off her phone to think.

Raven's bed lay empty, yet her she could see her car parked below the trees. Garnet imagined her with *him*. She wanted to shout through the window, 'Take care and a hex on that carnivore.' Cross-legged with her back to the window she heard dung beetles whirring on the sill, the shift and scatter of leaves on the paths, the growl of the dog on the chain. *Strange things abound*, she thought, *and I am one of them.*

She attacked her keyboard; beat up Raven in her journal. Did she deserve everything she got? Only a child would think that. The whole world heaped shit on solitary women. Garnet rose and surveyed the river paddock again where the fire now glowed amber beneath the trees. Chill slid under the window sash, slipped in from the valley, attacked her bare legs. Atmospheric warmth had moved on, away. The just discernible, hunched figure, faintly outlined in the moonlight worried her. Should she go to him? On her phone more messages had come in:

Ting

Zane: Come down.
Zane: Do.
Zane: Please.
Seven messages, much the same. And 'please'! Zane begging – uncharacteristic – on their property. The moon had moved, turned

steely white with dark smudges on its surface, distorted like a Dali clock as it slid in and out of view behind the trees.

Garnet dragged on her RM's, trackpants and a baggy top, and snuck downstairs and out the door. As she dashed between the rowans, the dogwood and the catkins, the neighbour's birds set up a chorus, nodding and bouncing on their perches, and the neighbour's dog barked as if distressed. Near the river, Zane came into view, lying back on his elbows, some distance from the fire. He waved a cup and beckoned her.

'What are you doing?' she called under her breath.

'Waiting for you. Why do you keep turning off your phone?' He patted the space next to him and she took it, eyeing him queerly as he rolled sideways and up on one elbow to face her. After brief hesitation, she allowed his hand in the small of her back, to guide her forward, and their lips nudged.

'Your eyes look funny. You've been drinking? 'She pulled away.

'Just tea, Garnet. I visited the poison garden and now I think I'm dying.' He tittered as he disengaged from her.

'That is such a dumb thing to say during Mabon. And it's not a poison garden. Why do you go on about it?'

'Mabon.' Zane stood clumsily and swayed toward a massive red gum. 'I feel hot. Here, drink some of my tea.' He pressed a plastic cup into her hands. 'Look at the broomsticks down by the river. We had a coven, truly-ruly. Now they've all flown away. Into the night?' He swept out his arm like a diva.

'Stop raving.' Garnet sniffed the cup gingerly. 'What have you been doing?'

'Partying, partying with friends.'

'Who, bat-brain?'

'Perhaps you might address me with more respect. I'm older than you.'

Garnet scoffed.

'Some of our mutual friends. Cody, Lyndon.'

Why should she be jealous just because *they* had answered their phones?

'Where are they now?'

'Well, Lyndon is delivering home some of my nice *other* friends, the witchy ones who had to be home by midnight, poor babies, and the lovely Cody... I'm not sure.' Zane struggled to stay on his feet. 'I am so stinking hot. I am going to wet myself in that river.'

'Don't be an idiot. You're drunk. And it's almost winter. The water will be freezing.'

'Eat, drink, flee, I can do these things. I'm turned up bright.'

'You're babbling. Where's Cody again?'

He pointed toward the road.

'They're coming back in a day or two. I'll help you with your clothes. The water looks marvellous. Tantalising. I do love hallucinogens. Specially mushrooms, the way they bring on dreams.'

Garnet felt annoyed that he'd got messy near her house.

'Go back into town.' How had she been even the teeniest bit fond of him?

Zane threw off shoes and socks and rushed down the bank into the water. 'Oh, my balls...! The temperature is glacial.'

'Zane, don't go further in. There's not so much water at this time of year, but people call this section "the rapids." I don't know how deep it is in the middle. I do not want to come and get you.'

'You don't understand, Garnet. I'm burning up.' Zane waded on, smiled beatifically and slid below the surface, rising hippo-like to take one breath, then sank in a cloud of bubbles, seeming to have forgotten her presence.

For a minute, she watched him, stupidly holding the sides of her head to block out her panic. 'Zane, come out. You're an idiot,' she cried. He seemed oblivious. 'Please!'

When Lyndon arrived in Zane's car she ran towards him. 'I can't see Zane very well. He's in the middle of the river.'

'Jesus!' Lyndon ran his fingers through his hair. 'What are you doing, mate? he called. 'It's bloody freezing.'

How much longer could Zane rise and sink before he tired and sank forever? Garnet had called and called.

Cody came drifting along the bank: bright smile, unsteady walk, her happy song wavering in the air.

Lyndon turned to Garnet, wobbled on the spot and said, in a low voice, 'I was supposed to take her home, but she wouldn't shut up. I thought if she woke up Lyn and Gord there'd be hell to pay.'

He turned back to face the river. 'Zane, get out now. Don't be a wally.'

Garnet thought of asking Cody to stick out her tongue but then forgot about it because she suddenly decided Zane had sunk. Faint and dizzy, she held her breath. After counting sixty in her head, she knew he wasn't coming back up. She waded into the water, turning her ankle on the unsteady river stones. Lyndon followed. The cold took her breath away.

Zane reappeared, a mushroom floating, a heavy lump of clothing, upturned in the deepest part of the river. Garnet braced herself against the cold and pushed forward against the current. Then trod water as she hauled Zane around by the shoulders and began to tow him. No struggle at least.

Near the bank, Lyndon waded out, white-faced, and helped her keep Zane's face out of the water as they dragged him steadily up the slippery bank, bumping and grazing his backside over stones. His sodden body seemed suddenly heavier. They flopped him onto the bank, rolled him on his side and turned his head. Filthy slime and mud caked his face. Garnet slipped her fingers into his mouth to clear it of debris – river weed most likely – and checked for pulse and breathing. Cody squatted down to watch, made inane comments, and plucked at Zane's clothes.

'Cody, stop being bloody useless and run for Ebba!' yelled Garnet into her face.

'My head hurts.' Cody moaned. 'And I'm so thirsty.'

The wind picked up and rattled leaves, throwing them up like clay targets at a skeet. The river mud stank of cow manure; magpies *loodle-loodled*; and lights flicked on in the cottages.

Lyndon bent on hands and knees to gag among the reeds.

'You drank tea too, right? And you drove with Zane's baby friends. Zero sympathy.'

He clutched at his throat and began to vomit. 'I must be dreaming. This cannot be me.'

'I'll start. You might have to help me if people take too long to come and cover me. His pulse is super-fast now.'

She lowered her face to pinch Zane's nostrils with her shaky fingers and blow into his filthy mouth. To blow and count in rhythm. Never, ever, had she expected to apply swim training IRL on a drowned body. Lyndon hovered, vomit on his sweatshirt, hands crossed ready to apply compression.

Was it the mercy of a goddess that two more steady breaths saw Zane cough? She tucked his arm across his chest and rolled him on his other side to hold his head forward, tried hard to keep her terror at bay. He made choking sounds and cried, spat up more of the river. Zane annoyed her, but she didn't want him to die. Especially not in her back yard.

Finally, Ebba appeared, lit by a storm lantern, and slung a quilt around Zane's shoulders. Shaken, Garnet knelt beside him, hands on her knees; she dripped water, and tried not to howl. Raven flowed in next, black hair spilled over her shoulders, bra-less, barefoot, red-eyed and swathed in a Tibetan prayer wrap. Hand tucked like a child's into the pocket of Branwell Kershaw's coat.

'Ambulance is on the way, Garnet,' Ebba said, one arm around Cody's heaving shoulders. Why was *she* crying? 'I'll wait here with him while you get some warm clothes and a mug of Milo up at the house. Take Lyndon too.' Nothing fazed Ebba. At Sappho, she saw everything.

Lyndon clutched her arm for support as they dripped awkwardly across the stones, shoes in hand, to the house. Cody followed, hollow-eyed. Dreamy.

The ambulance came and went. Soon after, Zane's mother drove in, hammered them with questions through the driver's window, then turned back to meet the ambulance in town. Gord and Lyn arrived to scoop up their daughter.

'I'll ring you.' Cody hugged her friend.

Garnet thought she looked ten years old when she lifted the hem of her tee shirt to wipe her nose and wave her other hand in a rueful, curly-fingered way. In the driver's seat, her mum sat beside her, ramrod straight like a jailer.

Ebba pointed her little finger in the direction of the river, night-clothes blowing round her knees. 'We are a household of women.' She put an arm protectively around Garnet. 'We have caused no harm.'

'I hope everyone else thinks so. Go back to bed, darling Ebba. I can't thank you enough for coming to help me.'

'Shero.'

'I'm not certain Zane deserves our good spells but... cast one for me.'

Garnet changed out of wet clothes, then walked with Lyndon back to the river, to make sure the fire was out. They sat beside the last, glowing coals. Zane had left his shoes and socks by the river gum, and Lyndon would return them to him later in the morning. And the plastic cups and two thick scarves near the fire.

'Are you okay?' Lyndon held her hand.

'Sure, I must be.' Garnet smiled. 'Tell what happened? Two parties? Or did I just arrive late?'

'He messaged me. Then Cody. Mick dropped us off, couldn't stay. Zane wanted to celebrate something but was too rude to tell us what. Cody seemed keen and I'm always mildly curious. Before we got there, he'd already been drinking with Year Nine girls.'

'I ignored his messages for a while. That must be how I missed out on boiling the billy. Then I saw the fire and lights across the river. Heard gunfire.'

'That wasn't us. Zane insisted I drive the girls home. Thank goodness you turned up. I worried about leaving him... he looked strung-out.'

'What happened to the billy?'

'I chucked it in the river. Dunno why. Wasn't sure who was coming out when everything went to shit.'

'Lights are always on at your place.'

He laughed.

'Did you try the tea?'

'Yeah. I had a sip. Or two. Cody drank more and who knows what Zane had on board. I don't think he will remember.'

'He was acting crazy by the time I arrived. Gaia, I am *so* tired,' she said, and suddenly began to cry. 'I'd better go up to bed.'

Lyndon put his arm around her shoulders but couldn't keep his balance and let it drop. 'Fuck.'

'He could have drowned, Lyndon.' Garnet wept afresh.

'I'm going to sleep in the back of his car for an hour or so before I ring my parents. Don't dob. I'll be gone before morning.'

When Garnet walked through the back gates, she found Raven pacing between the next-door birdcages, chain-smoking, hair a mess. 'Come upstairs with me?' she begged, touching her arm. They hugged. But then her mother kept walking.

Garnet dragged on into the house. Where did Raven go then? Back inside the cottage to him? The computer hummed, the clock flicked over numbers, perhaps a small dreaming face watched over her from the window. Garnet slept. When she woke, the clock had stopped at midnight.

Next day, Dr Andrew Pryde and his wife arrived before lunch to drive their son's car home. Zane's mother wore designer jodhpurs and a felt hat. Because. In the *country*. Mouth turned down. Zane would shortly leave for boarding school. After recovering at home. They felt let down. Dr Andrew's face fell into lassitude. He nodded once or twice at Ebba and gazed across the river. Apportioning blame?

Garnet pressed close behind the curtains, listened hard, caught odd phrases, words here and there, 'didn't know they were involved', 'terrifying night', 'no harm done' and 'hope that they have learned their lesson.'

Ting

Lyndon: Are you OK? Good sleep?

Garnet: Fine. I feel guilty he took our datura.

Lyndon: Illogical. Zane chose and he didn't entice us with tea.

Garnet: Did he bring you and Cody just to watch?
Lyndon: We hoped you'd come out. He promised.
Garnet: In different ways, he's cruel to all of us.

Garnet: Can we meet to talk about last night?
Cody: Tomorrow?
Garnet: You know what I want to ask?
Cody: I promise I'll tell you everything. Just not tonight. Will you be all right till then?
Garnet: Have to be.

Kendra: Zane's going to boarding school in the city.
Garnet: I heard.
Kendra: Were they drinking *chicken blood* out at your place?
Garnet: I do believe there was some movement in the soup. Witch cackle.
Kendra: Poor you. Will you go to Mick's eighteenth?
Garnet: Absolutely. Daisy too.
Kendra: See you there. I've got a bloody English essay to finish. Weren't those chicks hysterical? Do you know much about witchcraft?
Garnet: Not really. But '*though our hearts break, we cannot flinch; these are new times.*'
Kendra: I suppose you've finished *your* essay?
Garnet: My lips are sealed.
Kendra: Oh bitchful. I love you not.

Daisy: It'll be funny without Zane.
Garnet: Maybe better. Hope *he* can cope.
Daisy: I have such a guts ache.
Garnet: Me too and we don't even live in the same household. Freaky that.

. . .

Garnet: Hey Cody, I've finished my essay. Come over and celebrate.

Cody: Gord and Lyn grounded me. Quick flits to the main street. Only. Have I got something to show you. It's on the tip of my tongue to tell the truth. I'm sucking ice for the pain. Let's meet before school and talk.

Garnet: Zane's going to town. Boarding. I s'pose you knew that.

Cody: It's always been on the cards. This time his folks spat it big time. I'll have to learn to live without him

Garnet: I'll help you.

Cody: I know. I'm so zipped up at home, I want to explode into the world.

Garnet: You're cool. Kiss Zaney farewell and you'll rock it on your own terms. One day you'll be glad you don't come from a perceived dysfunctional household like mine...

Cody: Speaking of... Will you smoke hot rocks with me?

Garnet: I might. After you finish your essay. Will you be alright until then?

Cody: Hangin' in there, babe.

Garnet felt inexplicably emo. The big drama had passed. Without Zane stirring the pot, surely things would settle down.

At eleven pm, Cody messaged to tell her she was sneaking out the window with Kendra's cousin and some of his mates. They were driving to a party in the city and would return by daylight.

Garnet: Why do you need to go? It's Sunday night.

Cody: Cities don't close on Sundays like dead holes on the coast.

Garnet: Won't Lyn lock you up from now on, if she finds your bed empty again?

Cody: Small risk. If they ring, say nothing. I might do the pillow in the bed thing.

Garnet: How's your tongue?

Cody: Same. Sore.
Garnet : It's school tomorrow. What's one party?
Cody: I want to live. And I want to tell you I love you.
Garnet: I know. Reciprocal.

Garnet imagined that Cody's parents had turned off the telly at ten-thirty, after the late-night news update, drank tea in bed before they read a chapter of their library books and fell asleep. Not a clue. At four am they might have rolled over in bed – did they still kiss – because they thought their daughter was dead to the world? They would have been right.

At midnight, Cody stopped answering her messages, but no time to check a phone meant she was having a good time. *Too true,* Cody would have said. Garnet left three more messages and fell asleep. It had been a massive weekend.

When she woke at seven, all she got was a tinny message: *the Voda-phone you have called is switched off or out of range. Please try again later.* So Cody.

When the phone call came, a deep, dark well of pain opened inside her. A car crash – four teenagers banged up against a gum tree. It could have been any of them. All of them.

A wind, a cold wind has come. But this was not *The Crucible,* not Abigail acting up a storm. Much worse than the sudden appearance of a yellow bird, which could be disproved.

A lot of people rang around.

'Did you know her?'

'Not really well.'

'Hardly much at all.'

'You know, I saw her out.'

'Are you sure it's true? It might be someone else.'

· · ·

But it was true. Cody had died in the ambulance before it had even reached town.

A memory of when the four of them had licked around corners, screeched on two wheels, laughed hysterically, feeling glorious terror. It had made Garnet feel intensely alive, but what had Cody felt this time?

This time, had she experienced the same split second of consciousness, before her body took the crunch of metal, her face the smash and hail of glass, her awareness of accelerating towards the solid river gum that killed her?

Had Kendra's cousin slid the car in a spray of gravel, over-corrected, before he swung back to hit the trunk? Had life slowed... compacted into one last second? Garnet gagged. Rocking back and forth on her bed, cradling her phone, she listened to Cody's voicemail message, repeatedly, and wept.

Hi peeps. I can't come to the phone right now. What's going down? Tell me later. I'll be back soon. And then a stupid laugh.

I've slammed my head into a solid object, mimicked Garnet. I'm out of phone range. Cody sounded young and sweet. Alive. Like John Proctor in *The Crucible*, Garnet couldn't seem to cry.

A very ape would weep at such a calamity! Have the devil dried up any tear of pity in you? Cody's death had not been her fault... Had it?

Ebba held Garnet. Cross-legged on a cushion in the living room, her lap full of hand-dyed wool, Raven fed dark colours across the cross strings of her weaving frame as if nothing else mattered. And yet, she raved about Garnet named for *life blood, not spilled blood, that she must climb into bed with her until she was thirty-five years old and stay safe at home with her mother.* If everything were not so terrible, Garnet thought she might laugh out loud. Since Saturday night, by the river, her mother's mood had changed into a downward spiral.

All those years. Those dark times. How the bloody hell had Raven stayed alive? And Ebba who had recoiled from Raven's worst excesses, snatched the clippers from her as she went to shave her head, and entreated her with sleeping pills when she paced along the passage in the early hours of the morning.

For a few days, the neighbour came and went, and Garnet hid, but from then on her mother's bedroom door stayed locked. Likely hollow-eyed, Raven would tug at the curtains in her bedroom to watch his movements.

Garnet thought about number theory. *Chaotic, anarchic, random, one moment in time gathering weight and slamming up against another, dropping away.*

Clumps and clusters – like the funerals of young people in country towns – three in June, and then none until December. Logarithms or patterns. Just when you thought you were safe, there you were, wrong place, wrong time. Right age. No extrapolation needed.

Ebba said, in their day, kids didn't go to funerals. Their cars didn't go fast enough. 'I feared for Cody,' she said, as she stroked Garnet's hair. 'Never think it's your fault. No one could have befriended and loved her better.'

At Cody's funeral, high school students swayed in the aisles of the parlour, spilled into the foyer, crowded along the form seats, heads ducked together, sipped each other's tears, held each other hard when they heard about the crumpled bodies. It was a war, and Cody was wasted as surely as if she'd been hit by a sniper. While the young buried their dead, witch stuff had been forgotten. Surviving kids together, they drew rank, felt epic as well as ruptured.

'It won't hurt them to go to a funeral,' pressed some mothers. 'Give them a fright.'

'Make them think.'

'We don't want to fetishise death,' said others. 'They're dark enough already. All this talk about what they want at their own funerals.'

Cody lay inside a mound of flowers while they filed past, to toss a single bloom, a farewell note, a party invitation into her silk-lined casket.

Classmates stumbled over their words, sobbed, remembered the good, the bad, and the incomprehensible. Adults must have thought back to baby Cody, then the first flush of womanhood, the flying out to meet life and then the slap bang of her losing the lot.

'Let's go out and get pissed,' Daisy said to Kendra, pulling her jacket tight around her throat.

She didn't mean it, Garnet knew. They were being as careless with words as they were with life sometimes. They were angry. No one talked about boys doing most of the driving, or why.

If only she could find a rewind button, so that Cody could rise back off the ground where she had crashed in an untidy heap, unwind her arms and legs and head, and ricochet back off the gum tree, into a safe seat, beside a driver filling bottles by the mouthful, spitting pills back into plastic containers, and driving backwards from the city and home again, the moon moving over his shoulder into the eastern sky.

Garnet touched foreheads with Lyndon, squeezed his arm, and went home to gather up some threads.

Spreadeagled on her bed in the early evening, she couldn't settle. The funeral looped through her brain, bringing on bursts of howling, which she tried to cover with loud music. She thumped her fists against her pillow, pushed her face deep and held her breath. Almost always, adults caused kids' problems, living their complicated lives, but direct blame could not be apportioned for Cody's death and Zane's near drowning; let alone how he had dragged younger kids into chaos without foreshadowing the setup.

Lyn and Gord were strict, no kidding. But chicken; they had birthed and raised their daughter to resist with equal and opposite force. And egg; Cody was impatient, smart and unique – who wouldn't try and protect her? Country life was supposed to be healthier, simpler, surely safer.

And Zane's dad, ironically, cared only for his status in the town. How could he not know how people derided him, even as they doffed their hats at the hospital and in the rooms? Garnet knew little about his glamorous wife. Only that she drove to the city a lot to buy silver junk for the creamy house.

She sat up and rocked back and forth on her bed. Sudden dizziness panicked her enough to wedge her head between her legs and pant. Bad idea. Hyperventilation placed her in danger of blacking out. Holding the bedhead steadied her.

Cody hadn't been wise, yet they had got each other. Why hadn't she told her about the neighbour's photos? Which, after she peeled back her rage over his sneakiness, were rather lovely, natural compositions. They could have admired them together and worked out what to do. He hadn't even given her copies. But then she remembered. She hadn't wanted to tell anyone about the photo in which she and Zane had kissed.

Would Raven come with her to explain that respectful adults didn't behave like that to other people's daughters; that they asked permission? Of course, she would have refused to sit because she didn't know him and, so far, he had behaved like his predatory birds: desperate, greedy, ruthless. His ill wife must just be an excuse.

Garnet wanted to run away from her difficult humans, really run away, not just lace up her running shoes and hit the main road until calm overtook her. She jerked off the bed and stormed downstairs to tell Raven how she felt. About everything.

Chapter Thirteen

BREAKING OF CURSES: PURIFICATION

No dice. Raven must be striding up the hills or along the valley floor somewhere. Chanting, gathering, smiling into green nothingness. Garnet rifled through her mother's drawers and the Saratoga trunk, sorted, skim-read, pried, puzzled over pills and potions, a pouch of sweet-smelling tobacco, second-hand books and sachets of herbs. Curiosity drove her, to find out why, why, why?

Disturbing photos of her mother as a beautiful young girl in which, presumably, no one, not even her family had noticed her tears. Photography could be a cool, cruel art. Garnet fingered soft woollen garments that could have been hers, a tiny blonde curl in the envelope labelled 'first haircut'.

Such a happy baby, bald, swathed in cloth like a burrito, food on her face and later madly on the move – like her mother? School reports sung both their praises. Garnet's most recent had said 'intelligent, conscientious student, occasionally disconnected'. Raven's read, 'intelligent, restless, needs to apply herself consistently to achieve her full potential'. Zero photos of a father person.

At the bottom of the trunk, beneath a pair of ballet shoes, she found an ultrasound picture. Garnet sank back on her heels and sucked in her breath. Eight weeks' gestation. The due date was her birthday, or near enough.

A double image. Two sacs – two babies. The photo was clipped to a pink filing card with notes:

Twins are a bad omen. Portentous, like swans landing on the loch. Wrap the girl in rosemary and the boy in cabbage leaves.

Garnet sought out Ebba, reading the newspaper in the sunroom.

'Are you managing, darling? Quite a week.' She patted the place next to her on the faded, chintzy couch, covered with fringed throws.

'Hanging in there.' Garnet sniffed and turned her head away.

'You've been crying.' Ebba drew her down beside her, coaxed her head into her lap.

'Ebba, tell me this doesn't mean anything.'

'What doesn't?' Ebba straightened her specs and reached for the laminated photo Garnet held over her head.

'What happened to my brother or sister? Was it adopted?'

Ebba peered at the scan, pushing her glasses up her nose to focus. 'Where did you find this?'

'At the bottom of the trunk.'

'Never born. One of the wonders of new technology, that we know at all.'

'I don't get it.'

Ebba sighed. 'It often happens that way. One twin develops normally, but the other might fail to thrive; shrivel back and became absorbed in the womb. Same way geese weave dead goslings into their nest while they wait for the others to hatch. No one ever knew about these other babies until ultrasound.'

'I don't believe you,' Garnet said slowly. 'Raven is canny. Think of her recipes for menstrual promotion. I've read them. Tansy, evening primrose, and douche of parsley. Implantation prevention – buckwheat, elder, rue, Queen Anne's lace, smartwood – all out there in her garden.'

'No, I don't think so. Because you are here in all your fulsomeness.'

'I'm not feeling very abundant. I feel sad.'

'You've endured some tough weeks. I am filled with admiration for your strong character. Sheroic to save Zane.'

'I just don't know what I'm doing, but you're so very kind.' They touched hands, kissed cheeks. 'I love you.' Garnet carried the scan back to her mother's room and lay on the bed holding it up to the light.

When Raven slid in looking pale and ill, Garnet jumped her. 'Where have you been? I need to talk to you.'

'Just give me a moment,' she said, one hand scrabbling in the bedside drawer for Panadol. 'Please fetch me a glass of water.'

Garnet returned and held the glass to her mother's lips. 'I found your recipes for getting rid of babies, and now I've found my brother.' She thrust the scan under her mother's nose.

'Garnet, I know you're upset about Cody and Zane and everything. The last week or so has been beyond rough, but please listen,' Raven whispered.

'My pregnancy was unplanned. You know how I am, Ying / Yang, rock / roll. I wanted the baby – not *you*, I didn't know *you* then – to go quietly away until I was better prepared. For days, I stayed awake over-thinking, reading and worrying. Then I made a bad decision. I mixed up herbal remedies and drank them every two or three hours until I bled.'

Raven stroked Garnet's face. 'I felt terrible pain. When I realised you were still inside me, and the bleeding stopped, I was worried the lithium might affect you. Of course, I was only expecting one baby. The doctor told me that I had probably come to my senses just in time, and he sent me for a scan. I saw you both. One of you sucking your thumb. You both looked small and neat and perfect.'

'You're talking about me and my sib.' Tears slid down Garnet's face. 'What then?'

'I bled once more – not much. Then at the twenty-week scan one baby had disappeared and I was stricken again. Overwhelmed by grief. Fierce and protective of you. I did nothing, took nothing, drank nothing. Ebba helped me hold you safe until term.'

'Things have been terrible... Why didn't you tell me some of these things?'

Raven shrugged. 'Going back to look can sometimes mean not going on.'

Garnet leaned against her mother's shoulder. They sat in silence. After a few minutes, Ebba pushed the door open with a tray of dandelion tea and slices of vegetable loaf. Then slipped away.

Garnet chewed her nails until half an hour later when her mother returned smelling of smoke. 'What about my father?'

'He had left Australia for the UK on a Rhode scholarship. So, I decided not to tell him about you. Sometimes, when you asked me about a father, I didn't know how to tell you. I didn't want you to feel as restless and unhappy as me.'

'Raven, it's weird, but sometimes, when I'm upset, I see an aura. The light shifts, reveals a familiar face, a little boy I don't recognise, perhaps an image from a dream? The ultrasound image felt like an affirmation. That I'm not going mad. Do you think...?'

'I never close my mind to anything. But always be respectful. If the little boy chose to reveal himself, it may be to comfort you.'

'He often comes when I'm upset.'

'You see. Some believe that when you speak to an image in the mirror, you are speaking to your brain.'

'That subconsciously I remember him? That I project him because I miss him?'

'Perhaps.'

'We hardly ever talk like this. I wish, I wish... we could.'

'Let's try harder. No more, prickly teen or sad mother. You have good instincts.'

Garnet took a deep breath and leaned towards her mother.

'Will you come with me when I confront the Branwell man about some photos he took of me...? He spied on me by the river once, when I mucked up with friends.'

'I think I may have seen one of them. He overstepped the mark taking it without asking, but the pic was tasteful. You looked wistful.'

'No. *No.* You haven't seen them all. He zoomed in on me! He invaded my privacy. He left that pic on his coffee table where *anyone* could see it. I wanted to kill him!'

Raven dropped her head. 'I need to take better care of you. I'm sorry. You're growing up so fast.'

Garnet bit her lip in aggravation. The rush of blood tasted like iron filings and reminded her of the neighbour's first attack on her. She wiped her mouth with the back of her hand.

'Mother, no. Listen to me, please. When he first introduced himself to me by the river, I acted rude. Then he grabbed me and bit my mouth. He touched me.'

'*Jesu Christo*! I had no idea. I should have thought more about you. I don't know him well enough. Perhaps he's not himself.'

'Why would you say that? I'm your daughter. No excuses.'

'His wife is sick.'

'I know that. So what?'

'She may not live past forty, and her care is expensive.'

'Sad.' Garnet laid her head against the palm of her mother's hand. 'For her.' As she stood, her colour heightened. 'Do you ever wish we were more like other people, Raven?'

'I wish, you wish. Fling wishes at the moon. I'm sorry, Garnet. I'm terribly sorry he has hurt you.'

Garnet swiped tears from her face. 'I'm going to go now.' Briefly, her head dropped on her mother's shoulder. 'Later, will you take the tray back to the kitchen?'

Her mother nodded. 'Tomorrow. I'll come with you. We'll lay down the law next door. You're quite right to feel angry.'

Garnet trailed upstairs, Blu-tacked the scan onto the corner of her monitor, and thought about messaging Lyndon. 'Harm none' was all very well, except in muddy water. Lately, she'd felt so confused. Would Lyndon think the neighbour assaulting her a police matter? She swung back on her chair.

Ting: film no. 8

'A Pricking-naeword daedshesay.mov,' began downloading. Always, as each film arrived, the narrative became clearer. The cast more familiar, in a blurry, indistinct kind of way.

The same girl lay, sprawled across a table. Face obscured by cloth, another girl leaned over her, prodded and poked her leg with a small threading dagger. Then held the instrument up to the camera, before she plunged it into small blemishes on the girl's body. It drew no blood. Freaky. Or were they faking with a retractable blade?

Late next morning, Garnet ran along the riverbank. Ran too hard. Her heart hurt. As if it could make a difference. She missed Cody. She ran until she felt exhausted, slept through the afternoon, and then through the dinner hour. Then woke, heart thumping, nauseous. Felt messed up. Bodies always knew when something was wrong.

From between her bedroom curtains, she saw Raven spelling out a message in stones on the neighbour's doorstep.

NOW

Out he came. Gestured. Tugged her through his front door. Knees in her mouth, at the top of the stairs, Garnet tried to pluck up enough nerve to go over but wanted to wait until they'd arranged the meeting properly. Oh Raven. No. Not like this.

Nevertheless, over she crept. Face pressed to the crack in the sunroom door, she saw them, heads together, seated in front of his window open to the river. A breeze played in Raven's hair. As usual, she looked too lightly dressed, he unusually tired. Raven poured liquid from a jug, into stone goblets. He tossed pasta in a wooden bowl. Smiled sadly. Smoke buffered the kitchen alcove.

Even though she hated him, Garnet felt suddenly afraid. For him? What if something terrible happened to him? What if Raven had lost self-control? *Great stones they lay upon his chest.* If only she had the conviction of Danforth in *The Crucible*, or grown up with her twin brother, which could have empowered her to better manage Raven, rely less on Ebba, and still confront the man.

She crept back upstairs to read through her essay, now trimmed to a thousand and one words. Unfortunately, she hadn't squared the Paisley / Salem comparative braided essay thing with Drako, who would quite likely slash her grade for not confining herself to the question. Ebba would say it didn't matter, that the journey was the important thing, and that Garnet had grown from her work. Journey. Such a cliché. A worn-out metaphor. But maybe it was true.

At eight pm, Raven ducked her head around the bedroom door, dressed like a child, in flannelette pyjamas, a plait hanging down her back.

'He came – he went. He lent me his copy of *The Tenant of Wildfell Hall*. We'll organise a proper meeting time tomorrow'.

'A very odd book for a man. He probably didn't understand it. I want you to be careful,' Garnet whispered. 'Try not to hurt people.'

'I won't – I don't. I know you don't think I'm worth a pinch most days, but I love you.' Garnet gave her the benefit of – who knew what? – hugged Raven and thought about biology.

'Of course, nothing has been resolved.'

'Never is.'

Garnet felt tears welling. 'Well. It bloody well should be.'

Raven hugged her back. 'Together, we will try to set our world right.'

'Mother, don't name him in a spell.'

'You think me unethical.'

'With you and him, I worry about who is in control.'

Her mother kissed her.

At nine pm, Lyndon came by to watch a film with her. They hardly spoke. At the gate he kissed her hand. He'd left by ten, when the March moon shone full and clear and clean and looked like a portal to somewhere else. Grey clouds skimmed beneath its skin. Garnet wanted. Everything stalled.

'Someone has slashed the datura,' Ebba announced at breakfast.

'Beautiful trees have a right to exist without being ill-used.' Dark circles bruised Raven's cheeks.

'Did you sleep last night?'

'I tried.'

Who would do that...? Garnet wondered. Not Zane, or his father. Lyndon? Branwell Kershaw? Raven, in a leap of faith? Ebba, to bring healing? No. Datura were hard to kill. Garnet had read that, ironically, they were even hard to poison.

Matriarchal blood ran sacred – potent – its flow linked to phases of the moon. Blood could unleash power. It could be drunk for wisdom. Garnet had begun to bleed that morning, and her belly swelled with energy. She made a sudden decision to visit Zane.

When she told Raven where she was going, her mother pressed a crystal, cool against her palm, closed her fingers over it, ducked her forehead against her daughter's. 'I know his father, Garnet. Take compassion with you. Zane must be troubled, lonely, looking for his place.'

'He's clever, Raven.'

'Cleverness brings no peace. His father thought he should use his gifts better. I'm sure Zane would have if he could.'

'Why not then?'

'Did you ask Cody why she took what she needed from him?'

'I tried. Before she told me the answer, she died.' Garnet wiped away tears with the back of her hand. She needed to stay strong.

Ebba dropped her off in the main street, where she bought sugar-free gum, and walked on towards the lower riverfront. *Now we shall touch the bottom of this swamp.* His mother directed her to where he sat up in bed, trigonometry text in hand, dabbing at a cut on his face.

She gently fisted his chin and raised her eyebrows. 'Shaving?'

'Guess who decked me? The loving pater.'

'Not again?! You're kidding.'

Zane shrugged. 'At least I'm alive and for that, I thank you. And I apologise for my failure to read urgent signals from my brainstem. Like *flee, save thyself.*'

'Maybe the datura made it wobble.'

'It made me very hot.'

She slid in front of his computer and clicked on the task bar to lift his chess game.

'You don't fool *me*, but it's only chess. Why hide it?'

'The olds have turning into latter-day Luddites. They think I'll reach some critical saturation point and start planning a massacre for Hitler's birthday. I am persona non grata.'

Garnet began to skim his inbox. Cody, Daisy, Garnet, Kendra, Lyndon, Mick – all present – plus Paisley, kimmer@paisley.net.uk, mail returned. And everything felt suddenly very, very sad. 'You put the others at risk.'

'Not my finest moment.'

Garnet swung her head and stared hard at him. 'So, complete confession time. Start with jacking my hard drive.'

'Game's up. Shame job.'

'In the first instance, why?' She would not cry. Would not believe she deserved his harassment.

He took the hit. 'Okay, the jig's up. I was bored. But, no excuse.'

'You tried to frighten me. Hurt me. That's cruel, not clever.' Garnet clicked on Paisley mail. Found an attachment. Spun the chair away from the monitor. 'How did you know I was researching Scottish witchcraft?'

'Cody told me, but after a while it didn't matter. I'm a programmer. I could know anything I wanted about you.' He looked immediately shamefaced.

She held her breath. Of course he'd want to brag.

'Hacking requires persistence as well as cognition. You must have guessed you'd lost control.'

A part of Garnet probably *had* known that, but sad, sadder, saddest. Rougher than your mother reading private stuff. Humiliating.

'What did you trade Cody, for my username and password?'

'It doesn't matter now.'

'Not to you. Or Cody.' A wave of misery swamped her. 'You've read my journal?'

'I wasn't going to, and not very much. I was jealous of Lyndon.'

'You're such a creep.' She felt grubby, teary. Humiliated.

'My crack at intimacy.'

'Bizarre. To take more than I offered. Some kind of violence.'

'I tried to stay ahead of Lyndon.'

'He watched you watching me.'

'He liked you too.'

'So snooping, marauding cats and films. What else? The climate changed at school.'

'Maybe to begin with, I dropped a pebble in the pool at school. Like in *The Crucible*, panic smells. You should have counter-accused.'

Garnet gagged. 'You brought harm. To Ebba and Raven. And to me. Perhaps to Cody. You don't get to criticise the way we handled it.'

His head slumped. 'I regret it, if it helps. I was angry with my father, with Lyndon, with everyone.'

'You projected that onto me. Evil and inexcusable. Two technical questions, geek boy. I know how you made the films. I played around with Ebba's camera – sepia effects in the garden, little grabs. You dressed your actors in scarves and hats to hide their faces, to undermine the clarity, I know. But who were they, the bit-part, child actors?'

'Year Nines. Owed me money.'

'You're older than all of us, and you harmed so many people.'

His head slumped. 'Fair call.'

'And the hacking in? No nuts and bolts, but roughly. Through my email account?'

'Tried that, and your music site. I searched tracks I knew you had in sequence. Got a wee bit of assistance from an excellent hacking site. And from a Scottish dictionary. Want the URLs?' His voice crackled with emotion. 'I started in your trash. I felt dirty.'

'You *are* dirty. You've gotta get a grip.'

'I'm truly sorry, Garnet.'

'Your father doesn't read his monthly bank statements. Clearly. Now you'll close your account for kimmer@paisley.com.uk and he will never, ever know.'

Both hands lifted in surrender, exposed raw red bands on his forearm. Self-harm, or Dad?

Garnet pressed on. 'You pirated software preventing me reopening the mov-files to save them.'

'What will you do?'

'Do you mean, will I dob?'

'I'm already in so much shit, you may as well. Boarding school, here I come.'

'If you deal there, they expel you. It's a thing in private schools. Bad for business.'

'I won't fit in. I hope I might still see you on exeats, but I understand if it's not something you want.'

'You must feel bad about Cody...?'

His face reddened.

'Relationships aren't differential equations. You can't balance them out afterwards. You can damage the X.'

'You saved my life,' Zane said quietly.

'As it happens.' She wiped her hand across her eyes. 'Now do something good with it.' She rose and moved out of his room, walked along the passage towards the front door.

'I will.' He offered a watery smile, more like a grimace, and stepped past her to unlatch the door.

'Goodbye, Zane.'

'There's one more attachment. Sent this morning,' he said. By way of apology?

She shrugged.

Dr Andrew Pryde swung smoothly into the driveway and clambered out of his BMW, black bag and newspaper under his arm. He looked unsurprised to see her. 'Terribly sad about Cody, Garnet. Parents' worst nightmare. I'm grateful that Zane's fine.'

'Yeah, he looks a lot better than when I pulled him out of the river.'

A look of impatience passed across his brow. 'We're thankful but, in all fairness, your mother might reflect on why he ended up there.'

Garnet glowered. 'Yesterday someone slashed the datura. Did you know?'

'Raven should have grubbed it out years ago. Bloody dangerous.'

'Sure, Dr Pryde. And you take care of your black bag. Ebba says script pads are as common as batshit on the black market. A dollar a page. If you leave them around, anyone could just walk in and take one.'

'You sound like your mother.' He smiled, as if she should be pleased. 'Gutsy.'

'She has my back at least.' Garnet wasn't 100% sure this was true. She swung her gaze to include Zane. 'Perhaps you need to take better care of your son.'

Dr Pryde flipped her off with his fingers. 'You'll understand the difficulties when you're a parent.'

When she saw Zane's eyes avert, his body flinch, perhaps in dread as his father pushed past him through the door, she softened. 'I'll call you, Zane.' *So Raven, maybe you taught me compassion. Might be wasted.*

Next week, she would track down the Year Nine girls who appeared in the film clips and take them out for hot chips. Let them talk. And talk. And talk.

But next, as soon as she got home, she would cross the path to the second cottage and give Branwell a lesson on good manners, permissions, respect. If he photographed her again, she would report him to the police, and even though Raven liked his conversation and other parts of him, Ebba would support her granddaughter. So much ferment generated by unhappy men. So much making it women's work.

Chapter Fourteen

PROSPERITY: HEALING

All hell had broken loose. A forty-four-gallon drum propped open the door of the neighbouring cottage. There were stones scattered across his doorstep, as if someone had kicked them aside. His black scarf trailed over one of the drums, the tail of it dangling in a congealing pool of blood. Two men in black tracksuits and denim jackets were lifting metal cylinders, burners, and stainless-steel canisters into a white Commadore.

Garnet ran down the hall to check on Raven, who turned out to be watching them from her bedroom window, hands twisting the curtains. Garnet put both arms around her waist.

'He let the birds out this morning. The hawks killed the pigeons. Blood and feathers everywhere.'

'No surprise there.' Garnet could see the aviary doors swinging in the wind. 'Who are those men?'

'Plain-clothes police.'

'Where's Ebba?'

'In her room.'

Ebba was writing furiously at her desk.

Garnet tapped her on the arm, and she jumped. 'What's going on over there?'

She looked tired, small, defeated. 'The neighbour was making amphetamines.'

'Did *you* call the police?'

'They called *me* before they raided! I tried to warn Raven – that she should stay here – not go over.'

'Branwell?'

'Someone must have tipped him off. I *hope* not Raven. Minutes before they arrived, he let the birds go, grabbed the dog and flew out.'

'Holy Gaia. Is she alright?'

'I think she'd already made up her mind about him. I wish she would go back to uni and finish her Masters. The bookshop makes her morbid.'

'Ebba, you're dreaming. Not about uni but... Did she get stuff from him? Drugs?'

'I don't know. When Raven's manic she hoovers everything up. It's so perverse, because then it brings her down.'

Garnet ran up the stairs and logged in.

Film no. 10: 'wirreat.mov'. Paisley.net's server was back up and running. At least Zane hadn't tried to fake a crowd, but the clip unsettled her more than usual. Some kinds of truth couldn't be distorted by his tip-tilted research. The girl's neck was bruised, her eye blackened and she looked dishevelled. Garnet looked hard at her face, tried to guess the identity of the Year Nine who owed him money. 'Wirreat', the strangling segment, based on a procedure Garnet had read about, included sound effects, which made it grim viewing.

Had Cody been present when the girl's head flopped onto her chest and when they lit the pile? Such clever photography. Last week Garnet would have been desperate to maximise, rewind, roll back and check. She supposed they had used a hessian dummy shape when the fire began to blaze, but they had made one simple error.

Zane had panned the camera across the flames and up into the trees. In the last half-second she caught a glimpse of Raven's lurid-pink oleanders. And then she saw her old skipping rope tied around a branch. So that was what they'd been doing that night. Afterwards, he'd invited the others to drink celebratory datura tea. Perhaps the Year Nines had had a curfew. Cody may not have known anything about them. Garnet felt better, knowing that.

Light would return after the winter solstice. She and Ebba would turn off all the switches in the house. They would take a lit taper to every candle in every room. But at the next Samhain, when the line between things human and those passed on was at its thinnest, Garnet would put a plate of Tim Tams on the veranda in honour of Cody, play her favourite music, and cry. There was always the possibility, Ebba said, that someone might visit, but best not to disturb people in their most recent manifestations.

'Do not call them up,' she added. 'Leave the dead in peace.' On Samhains past, Garnet had baked pumpkin and gingerbread, placed silver frames of Grandfather and Nan Miller on the sideboard, set an extra place at table with an antique knife and beeswax candles. Over the years, Garnet had thought the rituals so much fun. Cody had changed the concept of fun forever.

Absorbed dyeing rushes from native sedge, Raven held tongs over her buckets and wound her timer.

Ebba smiled at Garnet. 'Put on your red jacket, Raven and come outside.' Garnet watched both their faces. As her mother stood, she smiled. Ebba placed a hand on both their shoulders and pretended to sag.

'Did you submit your essay?'

'Need to know basis... Okay, I did. I'll probably get a B-plus. Nice covers, no guarantee of an A.'

'Meaningless but... I'll cast the circle. We'll concentrate our energies, focus on our goals, and find a new pathway out of recent darkness.' They filed through the door, Raven leading, Ebba following, and Garnet coming last to catch the doors for all of them.

Yellow eyes elongated, body hunched, feathers ruffled, a Boobook croaked down at them from a river red gum.

Garnet caught up to her mother and took her arm. 'Where has Branwell gone? I didn't get my chance to speak to him as we planned. You didn't bump him off and bury him in the garden?'

'Columbia, to visit his wife in a hospice.' She winked. 'I planned to kill him to save you the trouble but he left too fast.'

So much for their joint meeting. 'Don't trouble yourself, Raven, harm done by him will return to him threefold.' Now she would have to leave justice to the goddesses. 'Three times bad and three times good.'

Garnet snatched the broom leant up against the side wall and began to sweep.

'I'm going to find my father, you know, and the musty old Millers. And I don't believe you could kill anyone.' *My baby brother was an accident.* These inexplicable revelations elated her, and she knew that she had already forgiven Raven.

'We could all go to Scotland,' her mother said, taking her turn with the broom.

Arm raised, Ebba scattered salt and walked clockwise around the chosen space between the two cottages, creating new energy. Her small wooden wand pointed North, South, East, West and Centre. The neighbour had flown the coop, and the three women could safely honour air, earth, fire, spirit, and water, love nature and reclaim their sacred place.

Garnet painted the air with a kestrel feather, wished Cody reincarnated, and order restored on the riverbank.

'Cast the circle thrice, Ebba,' Raven cried out, 'as sign of our love and connectedness.'

Ebba smiled. 'I am the crone, the keeper of dark mysteries.

'Never.' Garnet knew that Ebba had begun with the best intent, a spell that was good and true. Threefold good fortune would follow. After the ceremony, she left her dear women to talk and ran upstairs to her room.

Ting

Lyndon: I know you can't forget Cody, or Zane for that matter, and nor can I but... can we do some dirty stuff together, you know eat ice cream, play tennis, chase my dog on the beach, share books, read the newspaper? I'll let you have the comic pages first. Kiss ######

Garnet: Will you upgrade my AV software so *he* can't get back in?

Lyndon: That's a joke, right? I prefer reading. But I'll watch you do it.

Garnet: No more witch porn.

Earlier that day, a hawk had become caught in one of Branwell's rabbit traps and Ebba and Raven had watched Garnet heave the heavy iron contraption into the river. Ripples rushed out, splashed up against each other, as the wake sucked it to the muddy bottom.

Ting

Lyndon: Will you come downstairs? I'm waiting in your garden behind the broken datura.

Garnet: I see you. Anew.

Lyndon: I see you.

The waning moon had shown early in the sky, opaque, smudged dirty white by clouds, against a backdrop of pomegranate sunrays. Despite light rain, they had reclaimed Garnet's favourite rock by the river. Feet dangling, in the water, they toasted Cody with elderberry wine.

Misty raindrops fell on their interwoven hands.

'Do you want to talk about the macrocosmos?' Lyndon asked.

Garnet turned, and softly kissed him.

'Yes,' she said. 'Tell me exactly what that means.'

Acknowledgments

I am a Celtic descended feminist who by chance met and then interviewed students actively practising white witchcraft. They had no truck with the devil, only the good impulses of women's care for each other and in nature. My maternal-Scottish family, passionate gardeners who identified as members of the McAlpine clan, migrated to Australia in 1864, and I have drawn on some of their historical details to furnish my Paisley plot. None of them were witches – in fact, my maternal, settler ancestor was an elder and lay preacher, at Paisley High Church, Renfrew. Importantly, Garnet's story is fiction and none of the characters resemble anyone I know.

'Harm None' is set in the early twenty-first century on the land of the Ramindjeri clan and beside *Muwerang* or the Inman River. I acknowledge the privilege of living on unceded Ngarrindjeri land and my professional relationships with their generous elders, from whom I learned. I respect their historical and ongoing custodianship of their land.

In the runup to the twenty-first century and during its early years, I worked across the education sector as a journal-editor, Fleurieu Peninsula school-co-ordinator May Gibbs Writers in Residence Program, teacher and teacher-librarian.

While convening a Middle School 'Radical Readers' student group, I published in *Viewpoints: On Books for Young Adults* (2002). Students sparked my interest in teen/YA novels with their protagonists' authentic voices, focus on personal growth, strong ethics, and redemptive leanings.

In 2002, 'Harm None' [then titled 'Intent'], a YA novel, was short-listed for the Adelaide Festival Literary Award for an Unpublished

Manuscript. The prize sponsors did not then publish YA. Instead, they published my adult novel *Cleanskin* (2006) mentored by Eva Hornung. Eva guided me into the University of Adelaide Creative Writing program, for which I will be eternally grateful. Professor Tom Shapcott read this novel and took on my supervision, enabling me to complete my MA in under twelve months. 'Intent' was put aside while I wrote two more novels, one for my MA, followed by a PhD at Flinders University, where I became a contract academic, teaching across twenty-one topics, mainly children's literature, creative writing, and English. Sincere thanks to colleagues and especially Professors Richard Hosking and Jeri Kroll, and Dr Dymphna Lonergan who trusted me with gainful employment.

Over the years since, *Harm None's* three women characters, their cottage by the river, the natural and unnatural worlds conjured in the story, and the idea of connectedness and loss, tugged at my imagination.

In 2018, I sold my poison river-view garden and moved to Naarm/Melbourne, to live and work as an adjunct academic, on unceded land belonging to the Bunurong people of the Kulin nation. I published an historical novel *Unsettled* (2019) and, during Covid lockdowns, published essays, short pieces, and longer stories.

During 2023, I chaired and presented sessions with ASSF (Australian Short Story Festival), ICSSE (International Conference on Short Story in English) and read new work for APWT (Asia Pacific Writers & Translators) at Ubud Readers and Writers Festival. In 2024, I won the Creative Prose 1st Prize, AAALS (American Association Australasian Literary Studies).

Many people read early versions of this novel, for instance, Scottish Australian friend Marion McKenzie, brilliant and innovative writer Gillian Rubinstein and my daughter Gemma Fahey, as well as my late parents Elvin and Keith Crouch, who read most things I wrote. I am ever grateful to my then literary agent and friend Franny Kelly, who advocated powerfully for the novel. Apologies to anyone I have left out.

Most recently, kind colleagues and friends generously read this new version: Anne Casey-Hardy, a powerhouse writer of strong girls; Dr Sharon Kernot YA, verse novelist extraordinaire; Emily Lorentzen my target reader; and Dr Margot McGovern rising star and advocate for YA Oz.

Always, I am sustained by my writer friends' passion for craft. These writers include members of my book club 'The Adelaide Ladies Reading Group' (Lisa Johnson Bennett, Kylie Cardell, Danielle Clode, Kate Douglas, Hannah Kent, Sara King, Heather Taylor Johnson, Rachel Mead, Margot McGovern, Anna Solding, Jessica White), from which I am now mainly in absentia; my present writing group (Ruth Clare, Bianca Denny, Elisabeth Hanscombe, Matthew Roberts and David Sornig); and treasured readers for particular projects (Danielle Clode, Sharon Kernot and Carol Lefevre.)

Thank you to Jessica Friedmann for her gifted engagement with and editing of the 'Harm None' manuscript, and to Jessica Mudditt dynamo and hardworking publisher and writer at Hembury Books and her team of industry experts. At a time of publishing turbulence in which companies continue to gobble each other, book contracts keep pushing forward, and thousands of writers feel desperate to tell their story – can this ever be a bad thing – these two Jesses are positive and powerful forces for good.

Thank you to Brian Lynch who correctly recognised the shortlisting of this novel as a watershed in our lives, who gets behind my every literary project, and who believes that publication is the only way to get a manuscript off me and away from my tinkering fingers. And to our other keen reading children Cameron Lynch and Tiffany Grimwade.